A
STAR-FILLED
GRACE

A
STAR-FILLED
GRACE

Worship and prayer resources for
Advent, Christmas & Epiphany

Rachel Mann

wild goose
publications

www.**ionabooks**.com

Copyright © 2015 Rachel Mann

First published 2015, reprinted 2017
Wild Goose Publications
21 Carlton Court, Glasgow G5 9JP, UK
www.ionabooks.com
Wild Goose Publications is the publishing division of the Iona Community.
Scottish Charity No. SC003794. Limited Company Reg. No. SC096243.

ISBN 978-1-84952-442-1

Cover image © Krinaphoto | Dreamstime.com

The publishers gratefully acknowledge the support of the Drummond Trust,
3 Pitt Terrace, Stirling FK8 2EY in producing this book.

Overseas distribution:
Australia: Willow Connection Pty Ltd, Unit 4A, 3-9 Kenneth Road,
Manly Vale, NSW 2093
New Zealand: Pleroma, Higginson Street, Otane 4170, Central Hawkes Bay
Canada: Novalis/Bayard Publishing & Distribution, 10 Lower Spadina Ave.,
Suite 400, Toronto, Ontario M5V 2Z2

Printed by Bell & Bain, Thornliebank, Glasgow

CONTENTS

PLAYS, MEDITATIONS & REFLECTIONS   127

A THIN PLACE

That we might be something to you –

that the fog which masks
Dun I*, turns rock to ghost
and falls towards the shore
might be a kind of *yes*

That you might dream of us –

at night conjure pilgrims
in search of the hush and thwack
of water, the spit of brine
leaping from stones

That this might still be true –

that spectres gather in the bay
to listen for rumours of men
and women, winds from Labrador,
the whisper of the forgetful Word

But who could dare believe?

* *Dun I* is the tallest 'mountain' on the island of Iona.

INTRODUCTION

Christmas has become a bit of a problem for many Christians. As Christianity has receded from its privileged position within wider European and Euro-centric culture, Christmas – ironically – has never been more popular and universal. But, for many Christians, the version of Christmas favoured by our modern consumer culture is only vaguely connected to the religious celebration of the birth of the Christ Child. One doesn't need to look far to find the signs of the disconnection between Christian and consumerist ideas about Christmas. Consider the way the season of Advent has almost completely lost its significance outside of Church culture (and even within the Church). Equally, Christmas doesn't begin on 25th December. Christmas is effectively a season from the beginning of December (if not earlier!) through to 25th December. Even within churches, the tradition of not singing carols until Christmas Day has mostly been lost.

The truth is that Christmas has always been a curious festival, not least because many of our theological forebears have not seen it as fundamental to Christian identity. At the heart of our faith is the feast of Passion and Resurrection, Easter. The Easter Event is crucial to Christian self-understanding. The centre of gravity in all four gospels is towards the passion, death and resurrection of Jesus. Neither the Gospel of Mark nor John has developed nativity stories. As has often been remarked, many of the 'traditions' now associated with Christmas in the Anglophone world were bequeathed to us by Dickens and the Victorians or appropriated from continental Europe.

A politically and socially alert and radical Christianity will rightly question the conspicuous and exploitative consumption present in modern culture. I say that with caution, however. I am uncomfortable with a 'holier-than-thou', supercilious approach to modern ways of 'doing' Christmas. The truth is that – whatever those of us of faith say – Christians no longer 'own' Christmas, if we ever did. So our critique of post-modern ways of celebrating Christmas is likely to be mere clashing cymbals if it is made in a pompous, self-righteous manner that disapproves of feasting and joy. Rather, an interesting critique of conspicuous consumption must be predicated on a sense of how feast is placed alongside fasting and God's passion for justice.

I still think we have a special claim to what fans of superhero cinema call 'the origin story' of Jesus. And what an origin story it is. The biblical accounts of the Nativity of Christ are mythic in the best sense of the word: that is, they give scope for the reader – of faith and none – to participate in powerfully suggestive stories that reveal as much about ourselves as our pictures of God. If the Easter Event is the foundation for a culture's whole way of going on, the Bible's representations of Nativity have shaped and been shaped by our cultural representations of motherhood, infancy and so on. Indeed, they indicate how far we need to rediscover and celebrate what the late Grace Jantzen called 'Natality' within our faith and culture. There is too much death in our faith, a mark of the patriarchal obsessions of Christianity with 'limit' and 'significance'. A rediscovery of birth, the maternal and the power of the womb – in short, the 'Natal' – would, in the very least, offer a powerful corrective to our death-dealing culture.

The Gospel pictures of Nativity hold the space within them for the most sentimental and the most radical readings. The sentimentality is represented in the 'gooey' images of baby Jesus that are typically associated with primary school nativity plays or carols like *Away in a Manger*. The radicalism lies in the text's capacity to hold readings that emphasise Jesus' 'outsider' status. Much has been made in recent years of the idea of 'God being born in a stable'; that God is – from the outset – not a 'King' born in a palace, but the son of a peasant couple who become refugees, and so on. Even if that might – depending on how we read the Greek in the original gospels – be open to challenge, Christians need to wrestle with the radical poverty located in the origin myths of our Saviour.

This book aims to add to an already substantial body of literature that attempts to resource churches, ministers, study groups and individuals at a time when there is a genuine interest in fresh ways of telling the Christmas stories. It contains resources for Advent, Christmas and Epiphany and is alert to the distinctiveness of those seasons. However, fans of careful order beware! I have not been religious or zealous in keeping these seasonal resources overly distinct. I'm afraid I rather fall into the modern sin of letting Advent run into Christmas and Christmas into Epiphany. I can only ask your forgiveness.

The writing in this book attempts to steer a careful path between what might be called 'sentimentalised' and 'radical' readings of Advent, Christmas and Epiphany. I do this advisedly. My instinct is to read 'against' comfortable and sentimental accounts of the Nativity. Theologically I am committed to a radical understanding of the Bible which not only reads it through a specific lens – e.g feminist and/or queer – but also reads against those texts which do violence to the traditionally marginalised and excluded. Many of the resources in this book draw on that radical tradition. For – as I see it – God is the ultimate Other who comes into our midst to disrupt our comfortable categories.

However, I'm also keen for this book to be usable in a wide range of liturgical and study contexts. The skill of the writer lies in trying to create voices, characters, stories and so on that are mere ciphers for ideas. I hope that – at least on occasion – the writing in this book achieves a sophistication and simplicity that can speak to readers from a wide range of theological and spiritual perspectives.

VOICES OF ADVENT & NATIVITY

In almost any social context two related questions present themselves: 'Who is allowed to speak?' and 'Who gets heard?' It is one of the abiding issues in a patriarchal institution like the Church that some voices are privileged over others, sometimes in the most unconscious way. The voices of 'white middle-aged, middle-class men' have wielded undue and often crushing influence in the Church. This is no less true when these voices are physically absent. Their power and authority have been signalled in the language of our author-ised liturgies and who gets to decide on what is canon and so on. Subaltern voices – women, people of colour, working-class people, disabled people, LGBT*[1] people – have often been systematically excluded from religious discourse. Or if they have been allowed to speak it has been on terms set by the privileged male voice.

God is subversive and scandalous, even if the Church struggles to be. If the Bible represents one way in which God seeks to subvert dominant dis-courses, it is striking how often the subaltern voices break through in the Nativity stories of the Gospel. Women – even young women – get to speak and speak startlingly. Peasants and shepherds are given central roles. Out-siders 'from the East' play key roles in God's discourse.

This section, *Voices of Advent and Nativity,* attempts to play creatively and lovingly with some of the 'voices' or characters of Advent, Christmas and Epiphany. I trust that no one believes that the biblical accounts of Jesus' birth are factual. It would take a determined boldness to claim that his birth actually happened as described in the Bible. What we have, rather, is a won-derfully prophetic and theologically daring bid by the Gospel writers to claim 'Christ' or 'Messiah' status for Jesus. The genealogy of Jesus in Matthew's gospel, for example, is a clear attempt to show Jesus' bona fides to all comers.

Yet the Nativities of Christ remain 'truth-bearing'. They direct our attention to possibilities of the God-Who-Comes-To-Dwell-Beside-Us. There is something scandalous about this, yet this scandal is precisely what makes the Nativity such rich ground for art, literature and culture.

These monologues are attempts to tell the myths around the birth of Jesus in an engaging and theologically refreshing way. They can be read as a series of meditations, or as an extended narrative, or be used individually in worship. For use in the latter context, the worship leader or minister may wish to edit some of the longer monologues.

To attempt to give voice to any character – biblical or otherwise, subaltern or otherwise – is always risky. In one sense it is obvious to say that all the voices represented here are versions of my voice. That's simply the nature of writing. I am alert to the issue of 'appropriation'. That is, I'm alert to the problems generated by me – a middle-class, white woman – seeking to write in and through less privileged voices, even if those voices are located in 'mythic' space. I can only invite the reader to be aware of that dimension. In some ways any attempt to express lost voices is doomed to failure. Insofar as these monologues fail, I hope they thereby inspire the reader to interrogate the biblical texts and make their own creative responses.

---

[1] Many people will be now be familiar with the term LGBT signifying Lesbian, Gay, Bi and Trans. As the LGBT 'community' has become more nuanced other terms have been added in: Q (signifying Queer) and I (signifying Intersex). I use the * to signify how complex the queer community has now become.

O STARTLING GOD

When we use religion to control you,
when we use faith to serve our vanity,
when we use charity to save ourselves
from meeting those in greatest need,
O Startling God, come.

Expose our strategies of power,
break the childish armour of our fear.
Come, meet us as yourself,
naked and without defence.

Come, expose the flimsy glamour
of wealth, competence and dominion.
Come, give us courage to be ourselves.
Meet us and set us free. **Amen**

ANGEL (1)

Luke 1:26-38

She was so young.

Too young.

But it's not my job to have opinions. It's my job to deliver news.

I thought she would run when I walked into her home. It would have been the reasonable thing to do.

I've got used to odd reactions to my presence. But she was cool. So composed that at first I thought she was stupid. She looked at me without blinking.

But I saw it was her courage. Men four times her age rarely have her self-possession. She was nobody's fool.

I also saw the knife. The whole time she spoke to me – in even, carefully controlled tones – she held a knife in her hand.

It was just a knife from her kitchen duties, but it was capable of real damage.

She gripped it tight, ready to strike. I don't think she'd have hesitated to use it.

I asked her my question – 'Will you say yes?' Told her she was chosen and blessed.

She didn't seem very impressed. She kept me standing there as she sat down.

She laid the knife out on the table and studied it. She sighed like a woman twice her age. Who already knew what it would cost.

Something within me hoped she would say 'no'.

I felt a tear fall down my cheek.

She looked at the knife for a long time. Then she said 'yes'.

MARY (1)

Luke 1:26-38

No one ever listens to girls. Not in my world. No one listens when we have something to say. No one believes us when something amazing happens. No one believes us when we get used and abused.

I was by the hearth when it happened. I don't know where my mother and father were. Or my brothers. I was by the hearth making bread, little flat breads dropped on a stone. It was one of my tasks.

I heard a noise. I thought it was the buzz of insects. But it was feet on gravel. I heard a voice – an unfamiliar voice, clear; it could have been a man or a woman's. One word, 'Hello.'

And then a face poked in through the door. When I think about it now I think it was a young face. Beardless. But I can't be sure. I thought, 'Oh. You're beautiful.'

I wasn't scared when he – when she – walked in. I know I should have been. After all, the visitor was a stranger.

I should have run. But I stood my ground. And when she spoke – the more I think about it, the more I think she was a she – she was kind.

'Mary, I've got something to ask.'

She knew my name. She might have got it from someone, but somehow I knew she hadn't.

'Who are you?' I asked.

'You already know,' she said.

And I did. I knew she was God. Or her messenger. I knew she was an angel.

'Will you say yes?' the angel asked. There was fear in her voice. As if any answer might be the wrong one.

I had felt womanhood stirring in me for months. My mother had told me what to expect. The itch in my chest. The stab in my belly. The blood that would come.

I knew what was being asked.

I said, 'Why me?'

God shrugged.

I had two questions. 'Will they hate me?' 'Will they hate the child?'

God wept. I stared.

'Will you do it?' she asked.

I gave the answer I knew I'd regret.

ELISABETH (I)

Luke 1

'Curse God and die.' That verse had been stuck in my head for years. Building like a headache.

Not that I could ever admit it. It wouldn't be acceptable for a priest's wife. We're a righteous couple. We're chosen. We set an example and my task is to support my husband in all I do. We are 'blessed'.

Blessed in every way except one – children.

The shame of it. Even a whore can conceive. But not me.

At first we laughed. Then we said we just needed to find the right time.

'God's time.' After a few years we stopped talking about it. Then we stopped trying. We tried to ignore the gossips who talked behind our backs.

Sometimes I could go for months, years, without thinking about it. I was busy. I was an important person in our community. Zecharias was always busy. I guess it meant we didn't have to talk.

And then we were old. And our chance was past.

I should have let it go. But I couldn't. And I couldn't speak of my anger and disgust with God. With anyone. I couldn't voice my shame.

I wanted to curse God and die.

I was old and tired. I stopped sleeping. I talked to myself. In my head, the pressure built and built.

I started to hear another voice. Not mine. It said, 'Curse God and die.' A sweet voice. A girl's voice. My voice, from another time. Maybe.

Sometimes you cannot resist. Some voices go on for so long you just give in.

So I did. I lay down on my bed and said it.

Nothing happened. I felt ridiculous. I cried. There was no God. None that heard me anyway.

Can a curse be a blessing?

It's ridiculous to say I fell pregnant because I cursed God. But being honest unblocked something in me. It helped me to start over.

A new thing happened in me. Something impossible: The stirring of a child.

Scripture says that in the days of justice, your sons and daughters will prophesy. Your old men will dream dreams and your young men see visions. I don't think it says that old women will conceive.

But they say Hannah the mother of the prophet Samuel was ancient when she conceived. They say that Sarah was practically dead when she was promised Isaac. And she laughed.

Whatever, whoever, is stirring in me will be a sign of justice. For everyone who's ever felt cursed. Who's ever had to keep a respectable face when the world's gone wrong. Who has ever cursed God. Who never thought they'd laugh. Who will never conceive. Who need someone to call the world to account.

JOSEPH (I)

Matthew 1:18-25

Do I look like a fool?

I might not be shiniest nail in the box, but that doesn't mean I deserve to be treated like a pillock.

That's what I felt like she'd done. Mary. My intended.

She'd told me she was pregnant.

I laughed when she first said it. It would be typical of her jokes.

But from the look on her face – fierce, determined, scared – I saw this was no joke.

I stared at her and I couldn't speak.

I saw that she thought I might hit her. Or spit on her.

That's what made me angry. That she could think that of me.

I wanted to get out. I wanted to shout.

I kicked a chair across the room.

Mary stood her ground.

I felt ashamed. To lose my temper like that.

I breathed deep and said, 'Who's the father?'

'God,' she said. Artlessly.

I laughed again. A sneer, really. I didn't deserve to be insulted.

I walked towards the door. I'd drop her. Release the obligation. It was more than she deserved. She deserved to be publicly shamed. Stoned.

'Joseph,' she said. Just one word. 'Joseph.'

It was the way she said it that mattered.

It wasn't pleading. It wasn't full of tears. There was no fear.

It was gentle. It had authority.

It was her voice, but it was not her voice.

It was a voice that knew me. That was more intimate than a whisper in my ear. It was a voice – impossible though it sounds – that knew my body better than I could.

It was that voice that stopped me.

It was that voice which told me I should try to trust her.

It was that voice which helped me say, 'Yes.' To her. To God.

ZECHARIAS (I)

Luke 1:5-24

It's an honour to serve at the Lord's altar. Incense rises and it's a blessing unto us.

But the older I get the more incense becomes a sign that my own life is dwindling. The way its fragrance burns and rises and then dissipates. My life has dwindled.

I did my duty by my faith and by my wife. I played my part. But I was exhausted and old. And unfulfilled.

My wife Elisabeth is a remarkable woman. Patient and clever. Kind. But we'd never had a child. We'd tried and tried, but nothing. We're not bad people. We love our neighbours, care for the sick and the stranger. Each month her blood came and then we tried again.

Until we stopped trying.

I was busy and tried not to think about it, but I was ashamed. I am a priest. With no child to carry my story on. I swear people laughed at me behind my back.

I'd lost my faith, I think. I thought God had forgotten us. I did my duty and hoped that would be enough.

Incense is a curious thing. Sometimes you see figures in the smoke. Patterns. Sometimes the smoke dances. Then you tell yourself you're a stupid old man.

But I know what I saw in the smoke that day. I know what I heard. But I could not believe him.

I'd lost so much faith that when God spoke I doubted him. How was I – a man whose life had dwindled almost to nothing – to believe good news?

How was I supposed to believe my wife was about to conceive?

I could have laughed. But I was angry. Why now? When my life was almost over. When Elisabeth and I were hardly likely to see our child grow up.

I was furious with God and I told him.

And he silenced me.

I stepped out of the sanctuary and I couldn't speak.

I'd filled the sanctuary with song. I'd always had opinions. I was respected and sought out for my words. And now I'd been silenced. Like a woman.

I returned to Elisabeth and began to listen for the first time in decades.

ELISABETH (II)

Luke 1:39-56

To be old is one thing. To be old and pregnant is another. I've learnt to live with the first. I'm trying to get used to the second. I think I'm becoming adept at the impossible.

I shouldn't have been surprised, then, by what happened when Mary arrived.

She was barely showing, but I knew all the same. More than that. I felt our common cause. I felt our bond in heaven and earth.

Do women have special knowledge? It's always sounded ridiculous to me. But sometimes when we are alone, away from the noise of men, we find our own wisdom.

And Wisdom was always female. And the Spirit too.

When Mary walked over the threshold I felt my baby kick inside. It wasn't the first time, but it was still a shock. I was still getting used to the impossible.

And when my baby kicked he woke something in me. I stopped sleeping and saw the Spirit's part in all this. I saw how the Spirit was with Mary and the Spirit was with me.

That the Spirit had blessed us both.

Ours was an extraordinary blessing. A Trinity of Love – of Mary, the Spirit and me. A new glory coming to birth through us.

MARY (II)

Luke 1:46-55

And on that day when I sang – that day I met Elisabeth –
I sang of how my body was full of God,
and my spirit rejoiced in the Spirit and all her works,
for she was with me in my poverty and in my riches.

And I sang of how, even if I am nothing to the power-brokers,
if to them I am just a woman, just a child,
the Wild Justice of God had blessed me and holy is her name.

And I sang, and I sang, of her mercy – of how her mercy
will be lavished on those who dare to rejoice in her awesome love,
who dare to oppose the mighty and greedy,
from everlasting to everlasting.

For she has shown the courage of women and the toughness of mothers
and scattered the arrogant and overbearing.
She has upturned the thrones of the powerful and exalted the nobodies;
she has fed the starving and has shown her fury towards the mean
    and selfish.
She has remembered her people who walked in the desert,
she has remembered our ancestors,
according to her promises to Sarah and Hagar, Ruth and Naomi, Deborah
    and Jael
and their descendants for ever.

ZECHARIAS (II)

Luke 1:57-80

And what is to be learned from silence? What is to be learned from listening to a different voice from the one religion tells you is true? The male voice. The voice of authority. The voice everyone imagined God used in the wilderness to command Moses.

My time in silence has taught me to cherish a different voice. A voice with another kind of authority – ancient, comprehending. A mother's voice perhaps. That knows exactly where all of her children have come from. That will not sleep till she knows they are flourishing.

I have been blessed to hear that voice. A voice I've never really heard before. Mainly because I've been so concerned with my own. I've been making noise all my life and, finally, struck silent, I had to listen.

Listen first to the voice of Elisabeth. Listen to the sound of her changing body and the child that grew within. I learned the meaning of touch – of how Elisabeth's miracle was mine too when she asked me to place my hands on her swollen belly.

Most of all, I learned to trust the quiet voice of God that does not insist, but waits for us in the silence and gives us our true voice.

I learned that when I finally spoke my blessing – when our child was born, when our boy was named John, not Zecharias after me – I spoke out of a deep silence where all good news is made.

For God is faithful. She is the womb of us all.

ROMAN SOLDIER

Luke 2:1-5

They come to me to register their ordinariness.

That is the purpose of this Census. Not to show how much wealth there is to exploit. Not to count heads. But to demonstrate once and for all that we're in charge.

They line up in front of people like me and register their ordinariness.

They make a mark at our disposal. They are at our disposal.

These people need to understand that it is we who have the big ideas, not them.

We give them concessions – they can worship their puny god, they can keep their holy places 'pure' – but they are to be in no doubt what power really looks like.

These people believe that their god will deliver them. From what? Us, I suppose. They call us oppressors, exploiters, all the easy names. They talk of salvation and hope. Every now and then a few of them rebel. Because the weak like things simple – good versus evil, black versus white.

As if we're the enemy.

The true enemy is superstition. We bring civilisation and development. We lift them out of superstition. When they pray for salvation they are rejecting the light of reason.

They're fools. They line up and give their names and professions. Peasants, the lot of them. None more pathetic than the carpenter and his pregnant wife.

He stood there and could barely mumble his name. His wife shook with pain. It was a disgrace that he couldn't provide for her better. And her fit to pop, too.

Bethlehem. The City of Kings they call it. This carpenter was in Bethlehem because he was descended from King David. Or some such nonsense.

You want a metaphor for how ridiculous this country is? This city no longer produces kings. It produces scared little men and women like the carpenter and his wife. Pieces in other people's games.

I feel sorry for the kid this couple will have. To be born into poverty and superstition. It would be better if he were never born.

A VILLAGER

Luke 2:6-8

Hospitality. It's part of our faith. We're supposed to be hosts as God is host – to welcome strangers as God welcomes the stranger in the land.

As if it were that simple. A Roman told me once that in his language 'hospitality' comes from the same root as both enemy and guest.

Now that makes sense. Because there's nothing pure about hospitality. Someone always wants something. Can anything be freely given? Freely received?

I don't know why I ignored my instinct when the couple knocked on my door. There'd been dozens of them. All day, every day, for a week. Forced to travel for the sake of a census.

I was sympathetic, of course. The regime was making ridiculous demands on decent people. But I had nothing. I had barely enough for my own family.

I'd told most of these refugees to head to the camp at the edge of town. The conditions were terrible, but it was the best we could offer. Our community was overwhelmed.

It was late and when I heard the knock it was all I could do not to tell them just to clear off. Though not so politely. But they kept knocking. Demanding hospitality I thought. I thought of what my Roman friend had said about hospitality.

I went and answered and launched into my spiel. 'Sorry, we've got no room, blah …' The couple simply stood there and waited for me to finish.

They were so exhausted. The man almost wild with exhaustion. The woman – well, the girl – breathless. She was in pain.

I thought she was hurt. Then I saw she was extremely pregnant.

The man said, 'Please.'

I was angry. I felt manipulated. Couldn't they see I had nothing? Couldn't they get it that I'd had people like them banging on my door all day for a week?

They stared at me.

'I can't help. Sorry,' I said.

'My wife,' the man said, pointing at her belly.

I was sick of sob stories. I began to shut the door.

'Wait.' It was the girl. It was the shock of hearing a female voice that stopped me.

The women don't usually speak.

'Please,' she said. 'For the baby. Somewhere dry. For when it comes.'

I looked at her. She was a kid, but she was tough. She had nothing left except a determination to get the baby born.

I stared at her. Nodded. I showed them to a shelter out back. It was adequate. It was dry.

'You've blessed God,' the girl said. 'When he comes, he will bless you.'

MARY (III)

Luke 2:1-7

I wish I could stop it all here. Just now. Where it's only Joseph and the baby and me.

I wish I could stop it all here. Now that the pain is gone and the baby is out of me and I have him in my arms asleep. All of us knackered.

Joseph keeps smiling and weeping. I doze – dreaming I'm holding a child – and wake to find I am.

I wish I could stop it all here. Just hold the world back. To simply enjoy knowing this child is ours. Is mine. That he is special as he is.

If I didn't believe what I'd been promised, it wouldn't make any difference. I'd still say this child was God. As much as any child is God.

I don't care what he's going to become. I don't care if he's a god or not. I just care that he's here with us. He's made it. He's safe. And he's ours.

JOSEPH (II)

Luke 2:1-8

It's stupid, but I hadn't thought he'd be so light. I can fit him in the palms of my hands. If I couldn't see him, I'd barely believe he was there.

My son. That's what Mary says I should call him. My son.

And from the moment he appeared, as he screamed in his tiny voice, I knew he was.

What's happened is too big for me. For my world. Mary talks of God and miracles. Mary says this little one will save us all.

He's already done that for me.

I could have turned my back and let Mary go when she told me she was pregnant. No one would have blamed me. They'd have said it was what she deserved. She'd have fallen so far.

I'm still not sure what I believe. But I believe in Mary. And I believe in this child.

He is so helpless. He is so beautiful. Is this what it's like to hold God in your hands?

ANGEL (II)

Luke 2:8-14 (Genesis 18:1-15 & 32:22-31)

People are unpredictable. One day you're fed honey cakes. Another you're wrestled to the ground and expected to pronounce a blessing.

I thought I'd have to threaten this lot – this gang of grubby men and women who live in the wilderness and spend far too much time alone with animals. A rough lot, who see wolves in shadows, who attack first and ask questions later.

I thought I'd have to show them magic tricks. Lights in the sky. A heavenly choir. I thought I might need to take a sword to one of their throats.

Instead they were intrigued. I saw them delight in my black clothes and skin.

There's a reason shepherds have always been closely associated with God and the Kingdom. They live on the edges and in the lonely places.

They get how it is for God. They know God is most at home away from the palaces and glory. They know that God is at work in the dark and the dark is dazzling and beautiful.

They saw my clothes and my skin and knew that I was gloriously strange. They knew that God had come to be with them.

After that it was easy. No need for magic. No need for heavenly choirs. I strode up to their leader – an old woman with hardly any teeth – and pointed out the way. She nodded. As if in that moment she was in touch with the shepherds of old who'd spent long nights in conversation with angels.

She smiled her toothless grin and said, 'So this is it, then? The poor shall see God and God will see them?'

I nodded. She placed a hand in mine and said, 'Lead on.'

SHEPHERD

Luke 2:8-20

We had no business being here. Our place is out in the hills and wilderness. Or guarding the sheepfold.

The glory we know is seen in clear night skies, the stars uncountable. The goodness we know is in a job well done.

It gets cold out on the hills and everyone sees strange things. In the dark a bush becomes a wolf.

But I've never seen the stars become angels before.

But we have seen another glory too.

We know we're not always loved, us shepherds. Some say we're not respectable. Others think we're the symbol of God's love. No one ever quite sees us for what we are: women and men trying to do a difficult job, wanting a bit of respect.

But that's the glory of what we've seen.

Not the glory of a sky turned to song. Not the glory of the kings and queens of old. Not even the glory told in the Scriptures.

We saw a child. And the child saw us. That night we were not disreputable. We were not the symbols of Israel. We were just men and women. Because that's what a baby does.

He's not interested in anything other than being loved and cared for. He responds to love.

The parents let me take him in my hands. My unwashed and greasy hands.

I held the holy child and the holy child held me.

MARY (IV)

Luke 2:21-38

You'd think we'd be used to people holding him by now. So many people have.

But the old man and woman in the Temple were different. The old don't hold back. They're unafraid to say it as it is.

The woman sang a song, a song that I've sung inside since the first day I felt the child kick. A song of saving and promise. A song about the God who will bring justice to the poor and downcast.

Her voice was broken. She sang like one of the homeless who beg at the gates. Her voice was a whistle, but it was the best song. It was a song of mourning. Not for a lost lover, but for a lost Kingdom.

I'd never believed it before, but I heard then how blessèd are those who mourn.

The old man tried to be kind, but he had the subtlety of a hammer. His joy at seeing my baby was overwhelming. Almost mad. But prophets are always a bit mad.

Then he said my son would break me. That my son would be the cause of the rising and falling of many. He said I would bleed too.

I know something about bleeding. All women do. But.

I know no child is unalloyed joy. There's always a cost.

But my boy is a baby and I know God is love.

I thought of the woman's song. Of mourning for a world where the down-trodden are lifted up.

I thought of how it would have been easier to have said no to God's call.

I looked at my baby and thought, no matter where this leads, I'm glad I said yes.

SIMEON

Luke 2:25-35

A promise is a terrible thing. It's the mark of a bond. It's a guarantee. Think of what God said would be our due. A promised land. A land of milk and honey.

But the cost. Our ancestors walked forty years in the wilderness. Thousands and thousands dead. Generations born into slavery who never truly escaped. It's a terrible thing to be offered a promise of good news. To never live to see it yourself.

They brought the child to the Temple. It was just another day. Hundreds of people – priests, Levites, people in search of hope, beggars at the gate – everywhere. And along the edges of the court, the old folk. Trying to keep out of the sun and away from the flies.

I'd been coming here day after day for years. Ever since my wife had died. I felt closer to her when I was here. I could pray. I felt closer to God.

Closer to God! I felt close to God once. I'd been one of those enthusiastic young men who shaped their whole life around prayer and fasting. I prayed, as they say, without ceasing. I swore off every indulgence. And I knew God. I knew the God who led us through the wilderness, who is the burning bush. I knew the God who provides. I knew the God who keeps his promises.

I received a promise. A promise I wouldn't die before I saw Israel's salvation. Just to say it sounds ridiculous. To say you can receive a promise from God. It didn't seem so crazy when I was young. When life was in front of me. When I felt special. Blessed. I had news. Good news. And I tried to share it.

Time makes fools of us all. I grew up. I married. I had children. And life got complicated. The promise of the wilderness became a mirage. Just another set of words I couldn't let go. Just another way I felt I had to be faithful to an old self.

The older I got, the more absurd it all seemed. My hair went grey, fell out, my skin wrinkled and I wanted to curse God, or my own vanity or whatever, for daring to believe in a stupid promise. I started to think I only believed in it because I'd always wanted to be special. Different.

That's the thing about promises. They won't let you go. And so I started coming to the Temple more often. The Temple. Herod's folly. As if God were more here than among the lepers at the city gates or out by the banks of the Jordan.

But I could get here. I thought, if the Messiah is ever to come, surely he'll come to the City. Surely he'll come to make sacrifice at the Temple. Or tear it down for the vanity it is.

For years, nothing. I saw all the candidates. The preachers and revolutionaries. The down-at-heel princelings. The sheep in wolf's clothing. The criminals pulling a trick. The men who offer promises and get nailed up the next day.

And then a pair of peasants entered the courts with a baby. A pair of nobodies, the woman clutching a wriggling bundle in her arms. And I knew.

You see couples like that every day. Harassed. A bit uncertain. Embarrassed by the fact they can't afford the proper sacrifice. But there was something different about them.

There was no halo of light. No band of angels hidden to ordinary eyes. There was shock and sleeplessness and exhaustion, all the things parents of newborns have. I knew that look. But there was more.

Maybe it was the way the woman held herself. The surety. The steeliness. The sense she was carrying something more precious than gold or even a firstborn.

I felt a fool when I asked if I could hold the child in my arms.

Did I see anything special? He was quite scrawny. Typical kid of a typically underfed girl. There was no special twinkle in the eyes. He didn't show abilities beyond his years. He didn't raise his week-old hand to bless me.

He cried. And I felt the warmth of his tiny body. I felt how precious this newborn was. I felt like I was holding the promise I had received. And I cried too.

I felt like I was holding the one who would carry the promise, for us all, of good news for the poor and despised and unimportant.

I can now go in peace. He carries the terrible, wonderful promise now.

Part of me wishes he didn't. Promises are guarantees. And the good news he carries will take everything he has. It will take everything from his mother too.

But I have been faithful. I can die. I can take my last breath and taste the promise. And know it's good.

ANNA

Luke 2:36-38

When I saw the couple with their baby, stood next to Simeon, I pitied them. There is something so defenceless about the young.

I saw them and I saw every last bit of brittleness. I saw the mother – barely more than a girl – pretending she knew what she was doing. Standing there as if she wasn't totally out of her depth. As if her breasts weren't heavy and sore from nursing. As if she wasn't a mother for the first time. I saw the father – older, but no less bewildered. As if he couldn't quite believe he was the father.

Simeon – hunched and white-haired – made them both look like bemused children. He does that to everyone.

Except me. I'm older than all of them. I live in the Temple courts. I've seen revolution and compromise. I've seen a new empire rise and I've seen how our leaders bend over backwards to fit in with the regime.

Everyone calls me a prophetess. I think that means they're scared of me. People are always scared of independent women with something to say.

The priests and lawyers try to shut me up. Say I am a stupid old woman. The three words they treat as ultimate insults.

As if God treats the old with such contempt. As if women are second rate. As if my lack of a teacher's education means I could not know what was on God's heart.

In our leaders' eyes all of that is true.

I've never claimed to speak the truth, only to seek it. If I am a prophetess, that just means I want to see justice and mercy and goodness prevail.

I want to see a world where the poor are fed and respected and where the rich are held to account. I want to see a world where women and girls aren't considered inferior. I want to see a world where anyone who doesn't fit the neat ideas about righteousness of our leaders isn't mocked and spat on and thrown out.

I do not want to be tolerated.

I want us to know the outrageousness of God's love.

I shuffled over to hear what Simeon had to say. He rarely speaks and when he does it's mostly free from nonsense.

He talked of the child in his arms as the light to light the way of all people to God.

Well, even the smartest of us can talk rubbish. And when I peered in and saw the face of the child he held, I was sure he had.

It was just a baby.

Babies are nothing. Babies are weak. Babies have no power except to call out our care and love. What use is a baby? This one wasn't even good-looking.

That's when I got the point. God's point.

This is the baby of peasants. This child has nothing. No status, no power, no position. It can't speak. It relies on our love.

I saw that this is how God wants to work with us. I saw that this is what the Kingdom might look like.

I smiled. I sang.

HEROD

Matthew 2:1-8, 16-18

I'm not a monster.

It irritates me when people say I am. As if I charge through my palaces full of rage. As if I carry out summary executions in the kitchen garden. As if I'd have a servant killed just for looking at me the wrong way.

I have an impossible task. This land has no sense of itself. It's a series of factions. It's a family that's nurtured hurts for years. Like all families, it's a dangerous place to be. It needs a father figure.

Without me this whole nation would fall apart.

And that's without considering our overlords. Someone has to be go-between for the Roman regime and the people. Can you imagine how difficult that is?

Without compromise the regime would crush us. I am the compromise. I've given the people stability and economic security. I rebuilt the Temple. I keep the Romans out of the Holy of Holies.

What do I ask in return? A little trust. Some obedience. Perhaps a little recognition. A willingness to see things my way.

The visitors from the East were well-dressed, educated people in search of – as they put it – 'the true king'. With the temerity to imply that that wasn't me.

When you're in my position you sometimes have to have the courage to take the decisions others are scared of. That's what a leader is for. Leaders lead and I showed the way.

Bethlehem. City of Kings. That's where my advisers said a challenger might emerge. I offered the foreigners a guide, but they declined. I asked that they return to me with news. I said something about wanting to do honour to the child. It seemed the right thing to say.

We were all sophisticates. We knew this was a matter of form. Of course they wouldn't return. Of course I wasn't going to do any child 'honour'. When your position is as fragile as mine you take whatever measures you can to make yourself stronger.

I considered having the strangers killed. That would have been satisfying.

I chose to have them followed discreetly.

I needed to secure my position. My son would be king one day. I wanted no challenger, prophesied or otherwise.

So once the visitors had left the region, I left it to my personal guard to do what was necessary.

It was a difficult decision. I have children. I love them.

But this was for the good of the nation. This was for stability. This was to save heartache. Remember how God was forced to sacrifice all those Egyptian children for the good of Israel. I don't think God would have done anything different if he'd been in my place.

THE ADVISER

Matthew 2:7-8

It's my job to find the guilty. It's my job to supply sound advice. It's my job to know what the King wants even before he knows himself.

What I do keeps the people safe. Rulers don't truly know their people. I ensure the ruler has enough information to make a decision that will prevent a revolution.

The arrival of the travellers from the East called for diplomacy. The King was tetchy. Excessively polite. I could see he wanted these men and women asking 'for the newborn King of the Jews' executed.

Better to use them. Better to use the scriptures to political ends. Make God work for us for once.

Bethlehem. A squalid little town full of troublemakers and idiots. A place living on its past. Just because King David had been born there they thought they were special.

So that's where we sent the visitors. If there was going to be a pretender to the crown, if there was to be a rebellion, it was likely to start there. That's how it works – ideas of grandeur fill little minds with dreams. Peasants think they're the new King David. They hear stories of shepherd boys killing giants and think it's their turn.

What better way of doing our dirty work than getting foreigners to do it? Send them in to see if the rumours are true. Lead us to any agitators and insurgents. And if it all goes wrong? They're only foreigners. They're dispensable.

Let them believe they're on the way to find the true king. If they find their 'king' let him believe he's going to overthrow everything.

We'll show him otherwise. God is not with the fools. He's with the clever. God does not care for stargazers and dreamers. He's with those who are in charge.

THE SOLDIER

Matthew 2:16-18

One by one the stars were going out.

It had been a cold night. We practically hugged the fires as we sat around and ate and drank. Some of the lads got very drunk. Normally the officers keep a tight control on that. Not that night. We all knew what was coming. It wasn't an occasion for sobriety. Even the commander had a few.

For as long as the fire burned and the dawn refused to come we could believe we were just on an exercise. Training in the desert.

I watched the clear dark sky. I watched the stars and prayed this night wouldn't end. I saw constellations I'd known since I was a boy. I saw a sky that had never changed. As dawn arrived, one by one the stars went out.

I'd been proud to be part of the Royal Guard. Not just anyone gets to do that job. You have one role: to protect the king at all costs. At all costs.

When we were assigned the job no one was happy. No one wanted to think about what it would mean. But it was our job to protect the king and we were told our task was necessary.

A pretender to the crown was hiding in Bethlehem. Seditious elements were at work there. There was no way to tell between those who were loyal and those who were not. We were told to do a difficult job with dignity and restraint. We were told that if there was any doubt we were to be unafraid. God would know his own.

Experience has taught me one thing about violence: act and act quickly. And be as clean as you can. Do not look into their eyes.

We went from house to house and dragged the people out. We gathered them in the square. Some people tried to run off, but we were herding them like sheep. Those who fled ran into our back-up unit.

We gathered them in the square. The old, the fit and the young. Then we separated the infants. There were a dozen or so. Their parents screamed. The mothers struggled and pleaded. One man – the father of one of the boys – got very angry and drew a knife. One of our lads soon shut him up.

It went very quiet then. The people knew we were serious.

We separated the parents from the children.

I never understood why we had to carry out our task in front of the parents. That was a mistake.

Some of our soldiers got off on killing kids. They held the parents' heads up. They forced them to watch.

I did my job because it was my job.

The human body, even a tiny one, has so much blood. It is just a sack of fear and faeces and blood. Right until the end the boy I was assigned to 'do' thought he would be ok. That it couldn't happen to him.

That's what being human is. It's thinking it will all be ok, despite the evidence. And experience tells me it won't. There is no God, no God who saves anyway. Saviours are put to death. The stars go out.

A MOTHER

Matthew 2:18

God's blessing comes in simple ways. I've never liked the fantasy men. Who talk about the God of the desert, who love to say he's a pillar of flame or leads us into battle. God – if he's any use at all – is practical. He provides food and protection. He is a woman who sweeps out the house so that it's clean.

God's blessing is for home and hearth, not for the Temple. I always saw God in my children. In the care and nurture of family and friends. In the provision of bread and wine.

They call our home 'the city of kings' because David came from here. It's a modest place really. A bit like David before he became king. Before he was dazzled with all that wealth.

We keep ourselves to ourselves down here.

We had got used to the occupier's soldiers, but this lot were different. Some people actually waved when they came into town at first light. They'd been to Jerusalem and seen the royal guard on sentry duty. They were our boys. They spoke our language, shared our faith. For some of us they were relatives.

A knock on a door can be many things. A request for help. A signal to run.

He was little more than a boy – the soldier who stood there. Hardly able to grow a beard. He was polite – actually invited us to join the others in the centre of the village. We chatted as we walked. I knew his accent – south of Jerusalem. I wondered if I knew his mother.

At one point I thought, 'He's going to cry. He's actually going to cry.' I couldn't understand why.

I think you know the rest.

The boy soldier proved he wasn't so much of a boy.

God proved he was useless.

I learnt that there is no comfort. That there is no end to tears.

A CHILD

Matthew 2:16-18

Soldiers have the best uniforms. We always loved to play at soldiers, pretending to be David and Goliath, Jonathan and Saul. We'd fashion swords out of stray bits of wood. A small bucket for a helmet.

It was so exciting when the King's Guard turned up. They're not as smart as the Romans, but their swords are better.

There were two of them who came to our house. A young one and an older one. The young one was nervous and the older one a bit rough. The young one told the older one not to shout as they led me and my brother away. I'd been looking after him. I'm three years older than him.

The younger soldier walked hand in hand with my brother and me. Me on one side, my brother on the other. I asked about the soldier's weapons and uniform. The older soldier told me to shut up, but the younger one smiled. I liked him.

I've never seen so many people in the square. Lots of soldiers. Grown-ups and kids. The young soldier said it would all be ok. He said my brother and me would be fine if we stood together.

Then there was lots of shouting. I didn't understand it. I couldn't see my mum and dad, but the grown-ups were arguing with the soldiers about us kids. Then it got really scary. Kids were being pulled away from their parents.

I kept looking for mummy and daddy. I saw our friendly soldier. I thought, as long as I can see him we'll be all right. He looked scared too.

The older soldier gave the young one a nod and he stepped over to my brother and me. He said my brother had to go with him.

Because he's little,' the soldier said when I asked why. 'Because we have to take care of him.'

My brother didn't want to go without me. I asked why I couldn't come.
' Because you're too old,' came the reply.

I looked at the soldier. You're supposed to trust them, aren't you? He's a King's Guard. They have to be good men to do that job.

The soldier smiled and held out his hand for my brother. I said to the soldier, 'Promise me he'll be safe.'

MAGI (I)

Matthew 2:1-12

The religious love to talk of journeys and pilgrimages. It makes them feel better, I think.

I can think of few worse things. The journey we undertook was arduous, exhausting and terrifying.

Camels died. Servants abandoned us. Arguments broke out. We wasted time chasing rumours of good news that proved empty con tricks. We were treated with suspicion in a dozen villages.

The closer we got the more I wanted to turn around. That might sound strange. But what if we only found an empty consolation? What if all we found was nothing?

We had left our homes because of dreams and promises and prophecies. I think many of us were on the lookout to prove how clever we were – that we could read the promise of justice and a better world in the skies.

What did we find? A family with nothing, living in squalor. Trying to live with a little dignity. We found a child. A perfectly ordinary child.

That hardly makes it sound worth it. No one needs to travel half a world to find an ordinary child and a family with nothing.

But sometimes you have to be prepared to travel to see the ordinary aright. We had to lose almost everything we had. We had to travel to the seat of one kind of power – the paranoid power of a leader who could be terrified by a child – to see what real power looks like.

We had travelled from home sure of our own power – of our riches and vision and brilliance – and we arrived at the infant ready to receive good news. And we returned home by another route, no longer comfortable with our old certainties.

JOSEPH (III)

Matthew 2:13-15

It's the north that's made me who I am. It's been my education.

I see that now. I might be a southerner, but the north changes you.

They don't like 'fancy' southern ways up there. They soon tell you if they think you're a pillock and tell you to your face. They'll take time to talk and drop in without notice. And if they like you, they'll take you to their bosom for life.

We Galileans know we have to stick together because the southerners with money and power think we're gobby, feckless and seditious. They're right about the first one. And the last one. Probably.

But when you're treated as scum you learn to stand up for each other and you learn who you can trust.

When the stranger, the wise woman from out east, came and warned us of what Herod planned to do I knew I could trust her. Because she had the openness that you see in the north. Because she didn't have a position to defend. Her power wasn't based on money and pushing people around. She was like us – an outsider, untrusted by the elite, gobby. She might have been something back home, but here she was nothing. And she didn't mind.

So when she said we should run, I listened. She said we should get as far away as we could. She said they were going to run too.

I began to see then what it all would mean. I'd thought it would bring joy to everyone. That's what God does, isn't it? And Jesus was just an infant. The only power he had was to invite our love and protection.

I saw that we had to become refugees. Refugees from the fear and greed and anger of the powerful. I saw that our kid, our little gift from God, would always be a refugee. There'd never be any safety for him.

I saw that maybe that's how God wants it. Kings build castles and palaces to be safe. And they were never going to be Jesus' home.

I looked at this Magi woman and said, 'Won't Herod come for all the infants in Bethlehem?'

She said nothing and looked away.

MAGI (II)

Matthew 2:9-12

I've been looking at the night sky my whole life.

I've dreamed I've walked the length of the Milky Way. I thought, as a child, that it was the path to heaven.

Do stars tell us anything? They tell us about the visions of the powerful and ambitious for sure. Like 'Berenice's Hair'. A constellation named in honour of an Egyptian King. Or the Pleiades. The daughters of Zeus. Stars show us our dreams and our projections.

I have my own theory. They are just light. Light from another time, another age.

Light reaching us. Pointing the way.

That's what I thought when we saw the star. That's what convinced me to leave home.

That's what I found to be true. After the countless miles, the dead-ends, and finally our discovery of the child.

A star gives itself to show the way. It dies in its giving. It is the grace that has no concern for itself. It might be named in honour of the powerful, but it offers itself for all. And it pointed us to the true light of the world.

MAGI (III)

I always saw grace in the stars, grace breaking the endless dark of night.

Now I see nothing in them.

They pointed us towards the source of everything good. Now I can barely even look.

It's not just that I've got old. Though that doesn't help. For me, there's so little future left that only my past seems to come before me.

The point is – when you've gone to the source of everything good and discovered that that source is just a peasant kid, everything gets messed up. All you thought you had becomes nonsense. The palace you spent your whole life making is turned into a shed overnight.

He'd be grown up now. The kid.

He comes to me in dreams. A flurry of faces. Versions of that cheeky little face in the crib. In dreams I see him leading revolutions. I see him with an army at his back. I see him holding court among the great and the good.

I've always had bad dreams.

If this kid is the source of grace and all that, why should he live down to my fantasies? He was a peasant's kid born in a no-note town. And the last we heard he'd become a refugee.

If that is what God looks like, I don't think he's going to fit my idea of good news.

It's been decades and I've heard nothing about him. Everything's gone dark. But if he's God, if he's the source of grace, maybe that's how he wants it. Maybe it's time for grace to work in another way – not through the ancient light of stars, but in the dark of new birth.

POEMS OF LIGHT & DARK

'In the beginning was the Word.' The opening of John's Gospel surely offers encouragement to all poets. It is an invitation to anyone serious about poetry to properly commit to the service of language.

Perhaps – ironically – that's why it can be tricky for poets who happen to be Christians to articulate what religious or Christian poetry looks like. For it is tempting for us to want to use words for some greater purpose – for example, to serve 'The Lord' or express our love of God, as if we can ever quite do that. Sincerity can be toxic for poetry.

The poetry included here is offered on its own terms. It is not intended as utilitarian. I am not trying to propagate my faith. Yet, given that it is included in a resource book rather than poetry collection, it would be ridiculous not to acknowledge that it is presented in the awareness that it may be used in carol services, Christmas services and so on. Given that the poetry included here was written over a significant period of time, it also demonstrates a variety of form and technique. Some of the earlier poems were written with more of their attention given to liturgical use than others. It may be that they are less formed as poetry, but I trust they still offer something of value.

This section begins with a poem in the voice of Eve – a character referenced in the classic opening biblical reading for a service of Nine Lessons and Carols – and closes with two poems related to Candlemas, the date many take to signal the end of the festive season. In between are poems that seek to play with biblical and seasonal images. One – *Feast* – is dedicated to my dear friend Nicola Slee who noted, c. 2004, that I struggled to write humorously. I'm not sure I'm any better now, but it was her love and support, during my ordination training, that began to help me believe I was a poet. She inspires me still.

Finally, I want to thank my friend, the emerging poet Hilary Robinson, for inspiring a section of *Mary & Child*. Her poem *The Holy Night* is exquisite and indirectly influenced my poem.

EVE*

Fingers poked in through sticky clay,
plucking bone from cage,
the tip slurping free with a pop,
that's how they say it was done.

I remember another start.
A winter of tears and tantrums,
scratchy nipples, my chest gathering weight,
swollen like hothouse fruit.

My hips, too, dough spreading,
the moon a rip tide in my guts.
Waking to blood clotting
on my thighs.

I was dying then, no mother
to soothe my neck, take a comb to my hair.
No sister to make me secret rags,
say this is how it would always be.

Later, I discovered the lure of flesh for flesh,
his body heavy on mine,
his whisper – *let me teach you the meaning of gravity* –
as he thrust his way in.

And if I too choose the clay, the rib?
We make stories to survive.
And who would not want one of the old gods
to reach in and remake them from the inside?

* First published in *Bare Fiction Magazine* 5. March 2015

THE FRUIT

It came away like it wanted
to be plucked. That's what I said,
my heart buzzing like hummingbird wings,
scouring my mind for ways to stick it back up.

I held something new born.
Its scent was earth and trampled grass.
I held early morning in my hands.
Its skin split easily with my thumb.

We giggled as we squeezed sap
onto each other's tongues,
kissed to savour the last sharp drop.
Only then, the panic, burying the remains,

picking at strands in our teeth,
washing our hands again and again.
Scurrying off to the deep groves
to watch for his step. You know the rest.

I've no regrets about what was done.
But there are mornings when I wake
dry-mouthed, dusty-eyed, and see
the cracked scoops my hands have become.

Then I would cast all of you, my children,
to the jackals, just to touch its curves,
feel the juice weep through my palms.
To cradle it like a suckling son.

FALLEN *

For MSR

You tumbled into the dark and I held you,
awkward as a foal, a confusion of feet and hands,
demanding whisky and cigarettes.

I marvelled at the flakes of ice,
black as old snow, falling from your skin,
the crackle as you entered my bed.

At night I'd try to learn you,
mapped your shoulders and neck,
the planes of your chest, the stumps on your back.

I fed you roast lamb, figs, food with weight.
Asked you the only question. *Can you ever go back?*
Held a finger to your mouth when you began to speak.

* First published in *Under the Radar Magazine* 15.

FIAT

How easy it seemed that day he loped inside,
trailing leaves and grit, the pieces of autumn,
speaking of blessings falling like apples from a tree.

His hands supple at the piano keys – *Bach* she thought,
a prelude – loosening her objections like a dress.
See, it's as simple as this ...

As if all it took was *Yes*. As if all it took
was to sit beside him, press a single note,
let it sing.

ST ELISABETH ZACHARIAS*

Come. Beyond thirst, beyond tending,
where rose petals crisp, water greens
in a vase.

Move closer. Breathe my dust, my very flesh
settling. Be dust with me. Here where
we place the things we've gathered –

the china labradors,
the endless cats,
the *Cliff Richard* plates.

Isn't this how it should be? Piling
fold on fold, letting gravity pull
on our bones, till we can resist no more?

Don't touch me. My cells ache. My skin
so thin spiders fall through.
It would be a sin to hold someone else.

* First published in *The North* 54 2015

THE KNOWLEDGE

I'd buried it so far down,
in the cold room of hopes raised and dashed,
among the clothes I would have bought you,
the blue eyes and crooked smile I'd dreamed you'd have.

So far down the door was wide open
when they began to speak of children,
letting their voices travel down through neck, chest,
past navel, towards the memory of another loss;

reaching for the voice of praise
women knew in the first days,
the myth days, the song the furies,
that Eve, knew before it all went wrong.

Litanies falling softly on my hospital bed –
my eldest is thirty now, a child of her own,
my girl is six, drives me mad, but she's my life
– just the usual words

of mothers breaking apart
the standstill of an empty afternoon
with what has already
been achieved.

JOSEPH AND THE ANGEL*

In a room perhaps. Saw and bench.
Plane and chisel. The tools of the trade.

But – to his delight – a boy again,
trees still to be climbed,

not yet caring what's a mattock, what's a yoke.
Opening a window, just to let the bright elsewhere in.

All this time, the visitor's words,
insistent, the hum of bees brought indoors.

One question again and again.
Do you understand?

Knowing he should speak.
Marvelling at the cleanliness

of his newly-made hands.

* First published in *Under The Radar Magazine* 15.

COME THEN

speak, if you dare, for the silenced,
rage, if you will, for the wasted and abused,
soothe, if you can, the wounds hidden deeper than bone.
Be born and wail for your milk while your people weep.
Be born for the roughshod,
among labourers, grass-chewers
and the slack-jawed.

Breathe and wait. Breathe and speak.
Utter your Word, your tattered, wondrous Word.

GENEALOGY

Eve was the sister
of Lilith was the sister
of Sarah was the sister
of Hagar was the sister
of Leah was the sister
of Rachel was the sister

of Rebekah was the sister
of Puah, of Shiprah

was the sister of Miriam
was the sister of Zipporah
was the sister of Ruth
was the sister of Naomi
was the sister of Deborah
was the sister of Jael, oh, of Jael
was the sister of Delilah
was the sister of Hannah
was the sister of Bathsheba
was the sister of Jezebel

yes, Jezebel was the sister
of Abigail was the sister
of Abishag was the sister
of Esther was the sister
of Gomer was the sister
of Jemima was the sister
of Salome, of Mary, of Mary,
was the sister of Mary,
was the sister of Martha,
was the sister of Elizabeth,
of Junia, of Lydia, was the sister
of Phoebe, was the sister
of all the women whose names
never got sealed in the book,
whose names are not remembered here.

TO A WATER GOD

'In the beginning was the Word ...'

I want to trace you back through the line of a river.
From the end point: brown waves, engine grease,
the vast elsewhere. I want to touch your sores:
docks and rotting wharfs, cranes flaked to rust.

I want you on my palms. Further back,
when you zig-zagged, young and pissed,
jumped off cliffs. I want you. Fresh and cold,
your first day. To touch that first pristine word.

MARY: HER KIND

After Sexton

I have known the greedy looks of men
their black eyes frightening as night.
I've hurried, busied myself since I was ten,
refused their snares, kept my wits bright:
Lonely child, lonelier woman, hardened mind.
A woman like that is no one's possession, quite.
I have been her kind.

I have been a canvas mother to a holy child,
a carved idol, received prayer from all who can't cope.
I've been forced to be pure, to deny the wild inside,
been stripped of sex to make me fit for hope:
seething, febrile, confused, disaligned.
A woman like that gets washed out, becomes empty and mild.
I have been her kind.

I have binned the heavy blue gown
escaped the velvet prison, stolen a motorbike.
I've pawned for a rock of crack the heavenly crown,
shagged some hairy ape, luscious women, 'cos that's what I like:
I have refused your dreams, wasted my soul.
A woman like that is free, save your frown.
I have been her kind.

MARY AND JOSEPH

And they are coming –
not footsore   cursing a lazy donkey
but hidden   stifled and breathless
in the jackhammer hold of a container truck.

And they are coming –
clasping each other like childhood toys
soothing and rocking their prayers chattered
their bodies   hot as fingers forced into a fire.

And the child kicking and bloating
scratching her insides wanting out
of the pitch and roll of the steel belly
her insides aching for the promised land to come.

MAPPA MUNDI

Elsewhere a king is fed grapes,
fat as globes, wondering how
it would feel to swallow
the world in a single gulp.

An emperor savours the scent
of honeysuckle, studies his elegant
hands, marvels at their power to condemn,
compel, free. Indulges his greatest truth: *I am God.*

Men and women kiss, curse, cry and spit,
dream of riding eagles' wings. Somewhere a child
lifts his head, watches wild horses run
to the birthplace of the moon.

Here a thirsty mouth opens.
The girl stares down at it,
as if at a puzzle, shocked if this is the answer.
Stares in terror and wonder at what she has done.

MANILA NATIVITY *

If it happened here,
it would take a taklobo
to hold you.
We'd wrench its lips apart with a bar,
scoop flakes onto the quay.

If it happened here,
we'd fend off gulls,
settle you down to sleep inside
the shell's dreamy curves, proclaim you
our King of Scale and Salt.

If it happened here,
there would be a cat
tapping you with her paw.
A creature who peeps,
tests your warmth.

If it happened here
there would be drums,
a kid annoying her dad,
thrum, crash, thrum,
bang that skin for God.

If it happened here
there would be a procession.
Tee shirts for dalmatics,
sweat for incense, no Mary on a dais,
a kid leathering a drum.

If it happened here,
we'd place you in a shell,
watch you sleep,
watch you catch the light,
become our pearl of great price.

* This poem is based on a painting of the Nativity set
in the Philippines, included in *Seeing Jesus – Exploring
the Bible through Contemporary Art* by Nicola Slee
(Christian Education, 2005). A 'taklobo' is what a giant
clam is called in the Philippines.

MARY & CHILD

Not wanting to lay him down
in the wood and cloth. Not yet.

Just one heartbeat more,
pressing the smooth skin, the pulse

of warmth she gave him,
to her breast. One last time.

Before she sets him
where others may come,

squeeze his toes, touch
the curled-up possibilities of his hands.

Before he becomes
one more body.

Before the world crashes in.

GLORIA IN EXCELSIS

No trumpets, no choir.
Just one man. Lean as trimmed meat.
Winkle-pickers, drainpipes, a switchblade knife.
Keeping it brief. *Here's the news:*
baby, stable, take a lamb, vamoose …

He watches them leave.
Opens and shuts the knife, pings the release.
Tests blade against thumb,
licks the line of blood.
Wishes they'd refused.

FEAST

not for me, this year, claggy meat anaemic and dry
not for me cindered stuffing and parsnip *à la mort*

not for me, this year, sludged sprouts and peas
not for me oil slick spuds and last year's cranberry sauce

for this year Christmas will be
Diwali Hanukkah Eid Christ-Child feast all in one
this year to zalabia's oozing crunch my diet shall be undone
rugelach rugelach let me bathe in your melt
soufganiot tickle my lips with your doughnutty dough
oh aloo gobi gulab jamun muttar paneer come come
be my delight make my waistband tight hear my longing sigh

and, yes, if I must, for the sake of good form
I might, as it's Christmas, eat a mince pie

CHRISTMAS

It is winter   cracking under ice
It is snow   dancing to earth
It is sky   blue light through leafless trees
It is oak   bare fingers, veins, arms upraised
It is sun   low burning candle white

It is a gap   a space   a breaking
It is a giggle   a gurgle   a cry

It is the child

And unto him we are born

THE HOLY INNOCENTS
AS A JOHN FORD WESTERN

1.

Just another early morning,
the doors of the saloon squeal back and forth,

There's Lee Van Cleef *sans* moustache,
jaws clamped on a cheroot, narrow-eyed,

he knows he's never getting out.
The coffin-maker too, Lon Chaney Jr,

knocks nails into bad wood,
a scene in search of a soundtrack,

Max Steiner scoring minor fifths,
remembering the loneliness

of arriving in New York with empty pockets.

2.

Closer in, the stars. Jimmy Stewart,
the preacher, a man who prays at dawn

like all righteous men should,
who prays now for the grace lying

even in the most blackened heart.
And the man at the top: John Wayne (of course)

who plays *Ethan Edwards* as the Iron Law,
rests his gammy leg on the stove,

spins his spurs, eyes the bottle
of liquor on the floor,

wonders if it's too early or too late to start.

3.

Just another early morning,
the doors of the saloon squeal back and forth,

another wild night, brawls and whores,
whisky and whores, waits to be cleared up.

'*A reckoning's a'coming,*' says old Wally Brennan,
good old Wally Brennan, lent for the day

by Howard Hawks, no teeth, telling tales
of Keaton and the silent stars.

And the camera tracks down the street,
cutaways to girls with ribbons in their hair

playing dolls with Ma.

4.

A three-year-old son wants to shave with Pa,
their foam-covered faces, the comedy of it.

Pa slides the blade across his face,
Steiner tries a cakewalk riff, banjos and guitars.

And back on the street, serious now,
Chris the Cripple, they all call him that,

no one knowing any better, or caring anyhow,
playing a soldier from the war, the *true* war, the war

America still lives in 1954, Chris a metaphor,
still in that grey coat

which gave him pride and took his all.

5.

Finally to baby Oakley and baby Nell,
the tragedians, the secret heroes of the show,

and the doting moms, Mrs Nelson (the preacher's wife),
a Maureen O'Hara cameo, her costumes all red

to match her hair, '*They have to be red,
Technicolor, a symbol of something,*' she says.

And young Natalie Wood, years out from her own death,
a pillow up her dress, pretends to carry her third.

Shots of babies, nice babies, good babies,
white babies, no other babies,

framed against a vista of dust rising in the west.

6.

And the Clantons. Or Scar.
Or Liberty Valance. Evil. On its way.

They can't wait to reach this town.
You've seen it all before.

Herod as Jack Palance
working up a Best Supporting Actor

shout (*'At his icy best'*),
never winning though, too cold

they say, staring at the camera
as if he hates it,

which secretly he does.

7.

'May this day bring us love,' prays Jimmy Stewart,
a kind man, but tough (*he flew bombers in the German war*),

and he ruffles little Oakley's hair, as the outlaws
stride into town, check the barrels of their guns.

And Big John puts down the bottle,
wipes his mouth,

his face the face of a god, and he smiles
as Deputy Brennan jokes about *varmints,*

he smiles like a god who knows violence can be used for good,
who knows that no true catastrophe

could happen on his watch.

MAGI VAGANTES

'A bone, God wot! Sticks in my throat –
Without I have a draught of cornie ale,
Nappy and stale, my life lies in great waste.'
– Old Drinking Carol

In the version I heard, they weren't kings,
but beggars drawn by the rumour of drink,
the chance to warm their feet for a night.
And for gifts? They carried nowt,
but herpes and fleas and armfuls of rags,
singing *Tosse the Pot* and divers filthy tunes

while the good tried to sleep. Dance tunes
fiddled through the faded city of kings,
courtesy of *The Guising Company of Rags*,
as the old lags – desperate to score a drink –
rattled tavern and church door, turned up nowt.
(For who really welcomes sots at night?)

But beggars have hymns to Old Mother Night,
and so they sang, *Send sack and merrie tunes!*
Send comfort, ever wild and free! For nowt
in this vile lyfe, O Mother of Kings,
compares to thee! Grant skinfulles of drink,
send your star, your bright son, The Prince of Rags!

For when your world has been turned to rags,
what's left but a cup of comfort at night,
a fire and a few bottles of grog to drink?
It's no sin to be cheered by bawdy tunes,
to search in grubby places for kings,
knowing that palaces promise nowt.

Did they find the place where those with nowt
receive robes of grace, raiment for wet rags?
You judge. They found fire worthy of kings,
a family hiding out for the night,
and *The Company* sang divers raucous tunes
and all took turns to hold the kid. To drink

in the blaze from his eyes, the fiery drink
which fixes stars to the blackened nowt
of the skies, calls forth angel tunes,
makes you forget you'll only ever wear rags.
Tells you if life offers you nowt but ice and night,
sometimes in song you're warmer than kings.

In the version I heard, they were beggars in rags
mumming tunes for drink in the night,
pockets full of nothing, richer than kings.

THE FLIGHT TO EGYPT

I imagine them escaping in the night,
a donkey, two old sacks enough for everything,
not daring to look back.

Only years later finding out what happened,
the stories of soldiers breaking babies' necks,
the parents' heads held up, forced to watch.

I want to understand how they must have felt,
receiving that news, in idle chit-chat perhaps,
What do you mean you haven't heard?

New information forcing them to search back
through the years of safety, the blessèd good luck,
the two words – *get out!* – they'd treated as a gift.

Feeling it was all their fault, perhaps.
Knowledge carried between them,
a secret passed in glances, back and forth.

Never speaking of it. Looking at their son.
Recalling what they'd been told: how the soldiers
had held the parents' heads up, forced them to watch.

RETURN OF THE MAGI

They departed into their own country another way – Matt. 2:12

after we'd held the kid
passed eight pounds
of wriggling judgement
from hand to hand

after we'd placed our gifts
beneath the crib
had dreams of the other king
knifing us to save his land

we chartered a jet
split town
avoided the stars
scattered like grains of sand.

BAPTISM

Gasping he steps in   lets it grasp
ankles   waist   shoulders   neck
feels it cut his throat

wriggles and pulses
scatters skin in papery coils
glassy slough

flexes limbs   cracks knuckles
winces   searches for new things
sinks beneath

runs hands round the curve of hips
pinches skin   squeezes fat
finds folds to slide a finger in

opens her eyes
sees for the first time.

NUNC DIMITTIS

I take my turn to hold you,
feel you wriggle in the shawl,
know your warmth on my palms.
Just a newborn, not yet heavy

with words. I say my piece.
Empty my body of the last of the story
I've carried for forty years.

Your weight in my hands
enough to understand how grace
offers itself through the limits
of skin, a kiss, a pulsing heart.

THE SONG OF ANNA THE PROPHET

I'd like to find it.
Tucked into a monk's notebook
along with the filth:

manticores fucking cats, bishops as *Azrael*,
the *Whore of Babylon* sketched
from his dreams.

Little more than a scribble.
Against it in an old man's hand –
apocryphal.

Or just a stray piece of papyrus
in a pile of vellum,
a prop to balance a shelf.

Delectable mischief
Chrysostom, Origen, Ambrose
removed with a knife.

An old woman's words.
Knowledgeable. Made dry as rind,
flaking between my fingers.

An old woman's song,
going nowhere.
Unapologetic.

PRAYERS & LITURGY

Poetry and worship often intersect. One point of connection is the way both forms resist utility. They are often, in the most potent sense, 'useless'. That is, they are the kinds of activities that are destroyed when treated in terms of the effects they produce. Their value is not obviously measurable. Worship's value lies not in terms of its impact or effects; it matters because it is about our proper relationship with God.

These prayers and liturgical resources seek to add to an already substantial body of feminist liturgical gesture (to which Wild Goose Publications and the Iona Community has made an important contribution). My writing also seeks to bring a queer sensibility to bear on Advent, Christmas and Epiphany themes.

It seems to me that the Christian faith has always been significantly queer and festive themes bring that dimension out brilliantly. For at the centre of this story is a God who queers our concepts of power, authority and status. A young girl becomes the bearer of God and speaks with extraordinary authority. A god is incarnated not in the halls of power but among peasants and nobodies. In the Christmas stories, meaning and possibility are constantly played with; identity is reworked and redefined.

MIDWINTER PRAYER

God of all creation,
of bare forest and low northern skies,
of paths unknown and never to be taken,
of damp earth, bramble and sparrow.

We thank you for light, even in its midwinter failing,
we thank you for life, for its hope and resistance,
like a seed dying and living. **Amen**

COME TO US, STARTLING GOD

Come to us, startling God,
wake us from our ease.
Stir up our hunger for justice,
cast out our fear.
Open our ways to your ways,
lead us down the paths
of mercy and peace.

Come to us, dazzling God,
renew us with your love.
Tend our wounds
with your wounds.
Span the poverty
of our failures and betrayal
with the abundance of your grace.

Come to us, living God,
ever ancient, ever new.
Meet us in our sufficiency
and our greed.
Feed us with your compassion.
May your vulnerability
call forth our trust.

Come to us, disturbing God,
on our streets,
in the lonely places,
in the palaces of power
and among those without homes.
To restore, revive, and disrupt.
To comfort and convert.

O come, O come, Immanuel.

O ANTIPHONS

The 'O Antiphons' are responses used during the final seven days of Advent, after the Magnificat at Evening Prayer/Vespers in sections of the Western Church. These new antiphons may be used to replace the traditional Antiphons or be used in other worship during the final week of Advent.

O Sapienta

O Divine Wisdom, brooding mother, glory of God.
All are born in your grace and you shape the world
according to your mercy.
Come to us, and remake our foolishness,
grant us discernment and judgement
as we await the arrival of God's Child.

O Adonai

O Adonai, flame in the wilderness,
who delivers your people from our wanderings;
turn over the unjust tables of our world,
redeem and remake the structures of prejudice
which bind us. Liberate us through your love.

O Radix Jesse

O Stem of Jesse, tree of life and wonder,
bring forth your sweet and bitter fruit of hope.
In the shade of your mercy
is the promise of new life;

in your dying and living
is the birth of true freedom.

O Clavis David

O Key of David, O Peasant-King,
who breaks open the palaces
of the mighty and lifts up the poor;
set free our imprisoned love,
bring hope in our doubt and fear;
may your faith in us
teach us to trust each other.

O Oriens

O Radiant Dawn, O dazzling star
in whom the shadows of night
and the delights of day are one.
Comfort us in the dark,
illuminate us with your love,
bring your justice to birth.

O Rex Gentium

O King of the World,
you call the Nations
to a peace which surpasses understanding.

You who fashioned us
from dust and clay,
come and shape us into
your holy likeness.

O Emmanuel

O God With Us,
bringer of joy and delight,
come dwell with us soon;
save us, renew us,
remake us according to your Love.

A CHRISTMAS 'OUR FATHER' (REDUX*)

Our Father, which art in Amazon,
hallowed be thy games;
thy new releases come;
thy streaming be done,
in hi-def as it is in stereo.
Give us this day our daily tweets.
And forgive us for not spending enough,
as we forgive those who spend too little on us.
And lead us not into the food bank;
but deliver us from charitable giving.
For thine is the iPad,
the widescreen and the Playstation,
for ever and ever.
Amen

This is an updated version of a prayer that originally appeared in *Doing December Differently* in 2006. Such is the pace of technology, the original is obsolete. Please update as you find appropriate.

CHILDREN'S LIGHT PRAYERS, CHRISTINGLE

Please God keep people safe in the light. Please help people who do bad things to see the light – to be careful, to be kind, to find the way.

A chant may be sung. (E.g. The Lord is my light, my light and salvation … x3)

We thank you for light so plants can grow. We pray for people in places where there isn't enough to eat. We pray for people forced to grow luxury crops for countries that already have enough.

The Lord is my light, my light and salvation … x2

We thank you for light and heat so we can cook. We pray for places where power cuts make it hard to cook hot food and keep warm at night. We pray for people denied cheap electricity and gas because of human greed.

The Lord is my light, my light and salvation … x2

We thank you for the light in our lives that makes good things grow in us. We pray for all people whose light has been taken away. We pray for people who take away other people's light. God help the world be a better place.

The Lord is my light, my light and salvation … x2

ETERNAL GOD

Eternal God, we thank you for your faithfulness in a world and a church which often rejects. Shape us and all your pilgrim people for the tasks of justice and peace. Grant your people the courage to love.

(A chant/response may be sung or said.)

Passionate God, who walks with the excluded and unloved, who hungers for justice and truth, stir us now. Help us stand alongside the persecuted and abused and support all working to break the chains of hate, discrimination and injustice.

Glorious God, the fierce love of your Spirit meets us in our longing. Expose hatred, renew hope and dispel despair. Tend the deep needs of all, especially those who have been mistreated and rejected because of their sexuality.

Generous God, you delight in your creation and rejoice as we grow into your likeness. Refresh us with your presence when we are both fabulous and feeble. Bind up wounds of mistrust and bring peace to families, ourselves and the world.

Healing God, you gather up the fragments of our hope till nothing is lost. Bring good news to those who suffer in body, mind or spirit. May your Spirit comfort those who mourn, and the dead rest in peace to rise in your glory.

Outrageous God, who risked all to join us in human form, make us and all your pilgrim people ready to step beyond the comfortable places, that we might love both neighbour and stranger as ourselves. Free us from all that prevents us from meeting Christ in the other and the unexpected.

Wondrous God, fill us with that love which surpasses all and can transform the bleakest fear. Energise your people's lives so that we live for justice, mercy and peace. Illuminate our paths that we may walk your way of faith, hope and love in confidence and trust. Into your kingdom guide us and ever make us your own.

God of All, from love we are made and to love we shall return. May the sparks of our love and commitment kindle flames of joy and hope. May the light and warmth of your grace transform both us and our neighbours, both enemies and friends, both powerful and weak. Inspire us with the courage of your Passion – ever tender, ever strong – that we might serve your Kingdom both here and yet to come. **Amen**

SCANDALOUS GOD

Scandalous God,
you choose the way of foolishness.
Come dwell with us in vulnerability;
help us to discover riches
in your poverty
and poverty in our riches.
Disturb our complacency,
call us out into new life. **Amen**

BLESSING

May the world-making Creator God nurture us;
May the womb-made Redeemer God free us;
May the wayfaring Spirit of God illuminate the Way.
And may we go out
to be inspired and troubled
by the God whose love
is as tender as the cactus flower,
as sharp as its spikes.
Amen

CONFESSION: DIVINE OTHER

O God, wholly familiar, wholly strange:
We watch for your arrival, we wait for your approach:
seeking asylum, anxious for shelter, needy as a newborn.

O Divine Other, forgive us for the poverty of our welcome;
for the ease with which we fail to recognise your many faces.

O Divine Other, forgive us for the greediness of our need;
for forgetting your priorities and concentrating on our own.

O Divine Other, forgive us for the hungriness of our insecurity;
for the ease with which we become aggressive in the face of change.

O Divine Other, forgive us for the meanness of our vision;
for our desire to domesticate your presence.

Divine Other, wholly familiar, wholly strange –
other us. That we may be expectant and awake;
that we may confidently welcome you;
that we may be transformed by your dangerous presence.

The fragile and gracious Word forgives and transforms us –
We are forgiven. Thanks be to God.

HURRY US DOWN TO BETHLEHEM

As the Holy Child comes to birth
Hurry us down to Bethlehem for rejoicing!
As the Holy Child breaks into the world
Hurry us down to Bethlehem for celebration!
As the Holy Child awakes to the needs of the world
Hurry us to his side for transformation!

Though we have wandered long in dry lands
Soon the waters of justice shall flow!
Though the Star may have faded
Soon we shall walk in the company of the Holy One!
Though we have been a people lost in wilderness
Soon the Holy One shall lead us on the road to freedom!

Through the One who was, and is, and is yet to come,
We are a people of promise!
We are a people of hope!
We are a people of love!

Abundant God,
Flesh of our Flesh,
Food of our Hope,
Water of Life,
we rejoice in your arrival;
fulfil our longing for your love. Amen

GOD OF ALL GIFTS

God of All Gifts,
save us from hoarding the gold of our lives;
take the myrrh of our sorrow and heal our pain;
help us share the frankincense of our priestly call
with a world in need.
And the blessing of God,
Star-Maker, Wise Woman, Guide in the Night
be with us all this day and evermore. **Amen**

PRAYERS FOR JUSTICE

The voice of God cries out for justice;
The voice of God longs for wholeness;
The voice of God invites us into hope and love.

In stillness, let us seek to become
vulnerable to the voice of God.

We pray:

With people who only hear tormenting and oppressive voices raging inside their heads ...

With people whose voices boom so loud they think they speak with the voice of God ...

With multinationals and corporations, dictators and bullies, politicians lost in their own self-importance, countries which imagine they have a special calling from God ...

With all whose voices don't seem to count; whose mouths move, but no one listens. Whose cries can't penetrate the plate glass of our indifference ...

We pray:

For ourselves and all who are assaulted by a Babel of voices telling them 'You need this', 'You want that', 'Buy this product – you will be more popular, you'll be more beautiful'...

In silence we strain to hear the voice of God.

Silence

Out of the troubles of silence
gather us, Voice of God:
agitate and excite us
startle us with your unexpected presence
ready us to act for justice. **Amen**

PRAYERS OF APPROACH

Holy God, chuckling wise woman, tender and strange, we bless you. Bless us, trouble us, bewitch us into delight in your love, mercy and grace.

Christ our Sister, unite us in your holy bleeding. As you took spit and dust for healing, take our hands, cracked and huge as washerwomen's, for God's work. Take our sacred bodies for the healing of the world.

Birth-Spirit, as you coursed in intimacy through the veins of Eve and Adam, Hagar and Abraham, Deborah and Lappidoth, Naomi and Ruth, be the pulse of our lives. Desire us with your desire. **Amen**

BLESSING

May the God of anger and mercy
stir that beautiful, boisterous black angel
growling within you, causing you
to cherish who you are
and who you will be.
And may you find in the electric storm
of your life that eye of calm
crackling with energy enough
for you to resist
being stripped of hope, faith and love.
And the blessing of God,
Wise-woman, wound-mender, wildfire
Be with you/us all
this night and always. **Amen**

INTERCESSIONS (I)

In stillness, we offer to God the concerns of the world. Let us pray.

We remember:
Those who are without homes tonight … those whose homes have been torn away by natural disaster, and those, in a thousand different places, who will be sleeping rough. Anyone who can't feel at home with themselves. Exiles everywhere.

We remember:
Those who are feeling injured tonight … those whose bones and flesh ache for healing and those whose egos are bruised. Anyone for whom grief is as sore and bloody as a fresh-cut tattoo. Mourners everywhere.

We remember:
Those who feel they are mere scribbles in the margins tonight … those who fear violence because they look, think, act or believe differently. All whose backs and fingers are being worn out for the comfort of a rich minority. Outsiders everywhere.

We remember:
Those who are experiencing brutality tonight … those who are having their prayers and hopes drowned out by the sound of gunfire. Anyone who is trying to work out what they're going to do about the partner who keeps beating them up. Victims everywhere.

Vulnerable God
Enable us to stand by you in your hour of need;
Make us agents of hope and resisters of injustice.
Help us celebrate all that is beautifully strange within the world and ourselves.
Whether we are gathered, dispersed or scattered
like grains of corn in the wind.
Amen

INTERCESSIONS (II)

God of Light
help us to let the world and its troubles pray us,
may it be as if a flash camera is pointed at us,
illuminating your concerns, highlighting how we must act.

So we pray with:

All whose pain has been reduced, by our inattention, to a photograph in a
newspaper, destined to be thrown away tomorrow

All who feel frozen into a snapshot of themselves with no hope of escape

All who feel their lives are posed, grin fixed to conceal inner pain

All whose lives seem as easily wiped of value as an image on a digital camera

All whose anger bubbles like a Polaroid held over a flame

All who sense their lives are out of focus or over-exposed

All whose living seems as sepia and as ghostly as a photo from the distant past

Dynamic God, true image-maker, image-breaker, image-changer
help us hold up the negative of the world, full of possibility, to your light
that we may become agents of development and transformation
that all may celebrate the terrible wonder of your image. **Amen**

WHEN THE ROAD IS LONG

Wayfaring God, Companion and Friend,
when the road to Bethlehem seems far,
when the journey to adore the Holy Child is long,
come alongside us.

Show us the way to the stable,
guide us to the crib.
Grant us a glimpse of the glory
that illuminates the whole world. **Amen**

WHEN THE WAITING IS OVER

When the waiting is over and the child is born
When the shepherds have gone back to the fields
When the Magi have left their gifts and returned to distant lands
When Mary and Joseph have fled Herod's wrath –
Keep our hearts open, O God, to the call of your Kingdom. **Amen**

COME HOLY CHILD

Come Holy Child
greet us on our streets,
meet us at home and at work,
teach us to pray and do not hide from our need.

May your chuckle bring us hope,
may your tears make us long for peace,
may your arrival be the joy of the world. **Amen**

AFTER PSALM 141

God of Refuge, hear us now.
Let our prayer be as a lover's song on her beloved's ears.

Save us from self-importance, spare us the wine of brokenness.
Free us from the snares of loneliness and fear.

Keep watch over us.
Fill us with sacrificial love.

When we totter on the edge of despair,
hold us up on angels' wings.

Be our hope. Today, this morning, this evening, for ever.
Quicken our hearts with delight in you.

When the traps and tricks of vanity surround us, Refugee God,
travel with us. Be our passion, our hope, our life.
Enable us to stand by you in your hour of need. **Amen**

QUEERING GOD

Queering God,
remake and redeem your world.
Disturb and disrupt our easy pictures
of you. Come, smash our idols
With your fearsome love.

Queering God,
Empty yourself
into our comfortable world.
Show us the strange beauty
of your love, revive us
with your grace.

Queering God,
Reveal your wondrous truth.
Open us to a world
where you are eternal,
yet ever new. Wake us
from comforting certainty.

Queering God,
Come and dwell in our
exhausted world.
Show us your love
on the bitter tree,
in the garden of resurrection,
in a baby's giggle and cry. **Amen**

PRAYER OF COMMISSIONING*

God of the Dawn, Morning Star,
Mother and Father of All,
we bless your holy name!
Sing through your creation
as you did on the First Day!
Enfold your servant [...]
with your encouragement, hope and grace.
Inspire him/her and your whole Church
to embrace the wholeness of your Kingdom,
the promise of your love. **Amen**

* This prayer was originally written for Libby Lane, the first
woman to be consecrated bishop in the Church of England.
It was used as a prayer concluding the sermon for Libby's
consecration.

LABYRINTH STATIONS FOR ADVENT

One of the delights of the post-modern church has been the rediscovery of ancient patterns of prayer for weary pilgrims. Walking a labyrinth is a powerful and venerable prayer tradition. Modern cathedrals like Grace Cathedral in San Francisco and countless churches, including St Nicholas Burnage where I serve, have created permanent or temporary labyrinths after the pattern of the one in Chartres Cathedral or based on classical design. Information about making a labyrinth can be found here:

https://labyrinthsociety.org/download-a-labyrinth

The principle of a labyrinth (unlike a maze) is that there is only one path to the centre and one path out. Walking a labyrinth is a way of taking a journey into the centre of oneself, a story and God.

A few years ago when St Nick's created a labyrinth I wrote some 'prayer stations' for people travelling the 'road' of Advent towards the Christ Child. I was stunned by how powerful these simple prayer stations were for pilgrims. They are predicated on allowing people time to travel the path, pause and reflect.

These prayer stations should be written on card for individual pilgrims to read as they walk the labyrinth.

A labyrinth prayer

The labyrinth is ultimately a journey – a journey towards God our Centre and back out towards the world where we must live. It is one of the most ancient ways of prayer and has been part of Christian practice since at least the Middle Ages, though some would wish to trace its use right back to the earliest church.

Before entering the labyrinth, take off your shoes, stand still and breathe deeply.

Prepare yourself for a journey into God.

Recognise that as you enter the labyrinth you are treading on holy ground.

When you enter, do not hurry but take your time. God is waiting to meet you as you travel.

A prayer as you prepare to enter the labyrinth

God of the Journey,
may you meet me here
as I walk Holy Ground.
May I open my heart and mind
to your Spirit as I travel towards the Centre.
Amen

Preparation: hand-washing

Resources: A bowl of water at the entrance to the labyrinth

'A voice cries out ... Prepare the Way of the Lord' (Isaiah 40:3)

You are about to step into a special place ... onto holy ground. People have always used water to clean and prepare themselves for special things.

As you get ready to enter and walk the labyrinth, you are invited to place your hands in the water and then make the sign of the Cross on your forehead. Pray that God will help you walk alongside Mary and Joseph to Bethlehem.

Station 1: An angel comes to Mary and brings good news

Resources: A box containing feathers

The angel Gabriel came to a young woman called Mary who was not yet married. And the angel said to Mary: 'Do not be afraid ... soon you will have a son and you will name him Jesus. And he will be great. He will be the Son of God.'

Angels are God's special messengers. Sometimes we think of angels as having wings to fly.

Place your hands in the feathers and pray for all those who bring good news, or special news or happy news.

Ask God to help you be someone who shares good news with others. What good news do you have?

Station 2: Mary and Joseph go to Bethlehem

Resources: a pile of cloth strips

Mary and Joseph made the long and difficult journey from Nazareth to Bethlehem. Mary was pregnant and Joseph was engaged to be married to her. When they got to Bethlehem Mary gave birth to her son, Jesus.

Take one of the pieces of cloth. Carry it with you as you walk the labyrinth. This piece of cloth will be your offering for Jesus' cradle.

As you hold it, pray for those who are forced to travel very long distances, maybe to escape a difficult life. Pray for those who have very little and for those who feel they have little to offer.

Station 3: With the shepherds in the fields

Resources: A simple hand-held 'loom' and pieces of wool

While Mary, Joseph and Jesus were at Bethlehem, there were some shepherds in the fields. Suddenly an angel appeared to them. The shepherds were afraid, but the angel said, 'I bring you good news for everyone. Today is born in Bethlehem the

Son of God. You will find him wrapped in bands of cloth and lying in a manger.' The shepherds hurried down to Bethlehem to see the babe.

Take a piece of wool – the coat of a sheep – and thread it through this small loom. As you do so, think of this thread as being you – your life being threaded into the story of the shepherds. Remember that shepherds weren't always terribly popular in Jesus' time ... so pray for those whom you don't like, for those who are outcast or unpopular, whom no one likes but whom God still loves. We thread our lives with theirs in God's love ...

Station 4: With the Wise Men travelling to Bethlehem

Resources: A pile of chocolate coins wrapped in gold paper, a small bottle of frankincense essential oil, a small bottle of myrrh-scented oil.

While Jesus was in Bethlehem, Wise Men followed a star that was a sign of the birth of the King of the Jews, the Son of God. They came to Jesus and worshipped him, giving him great gifts of gold, frankincense and myrrh.

Take a gold coin and hold it in your hand – gold, the sign of royalty and wealth: pray for people who have big and difficult decisions to make.

Put some frankincense – a sign of priests and the Church – on the strip of cloth you were given. Sniff and savour the scent of the oil. Pray for the Church and people who try to love and serve God.

Put some myrrh – a perfume used to anoint the dead – on the strip of cloth. Take in the scents of the oil ... pray for those we have lost and miss or for those people who have lost someone and mourn.

Centre: The cradle of Jesus Christ

Resources: a box/crate, some straw, perhaps an electric light concealed beneath the straw to create a light effect. Some pens/crayons. Some handmade cardboard stars with a loop of string.

So Mary gave birth to a son, Jesus. And he was laid in a manger wrapped in simple bands of cloth. And he was 'Emmanuel' – 'God with us' – the Son of God, the Messiah. And shepherds and wise men came to honour him.

On the piece of cloth you were given, write a prayer for the world, or for yourself or for someone you love. Place your scrap of cloth, as your offering, in the cradle ...

Receive a star to place on your tree, a sign of the hope you take away.

A prayer at the centre of the labyrinth

God of the Journey,
help me to wait upon your love
as I come to the Centre.
May you help me
lay down my burdens and troubles
and receive the fullness of your grace.
Lead me out into the world
to serve your Kingdom.
Amen

A prayer as you leave the labyrinth

God of the Journey,
Thank you for being with me
in all I do –
in my joy and my pain,
in my waking and my rest,
at my beginning and at my end.
Lead me from here
filled with your Spirit
ready to serve you in faith, hope and love. **Amen**

WHEN WE HAVE WAITED LONG

When your promises seem empty,
when faith has grown tired and old,
dazzle us with your darkness and light,
illuminate the Way of Faith and Hope.
Restore us through your love,
and when our work is done,
gather us to yourself and grant us peace. **Amen**

PLAYS, MEDITATIONS
& REFLECTIONS

One of the things I remember fondly from growing up in the UK in the 1970s is nativity plays. They provided an opportunity for the talented and the untalented to dress up in tea towels and sheets and retell the birth stories of Jesus. I was lucky if I ever got to play second donkey, but they were a crucial part of getting me into drama and writing in later life.

Nativity plays are stereotyped as opportunities for parents to 'coo' and 'ooh' and 'aah' over their wee ones treading the boards for the first time. They are wrapped up in layers of sentimentality and no one especially minds if the acting is terrible or the bairns go off script. In recent years, schools have been accused of watering down the religious elements. Indeed, due to the understandable desire to include as many children as possible, characters as 'non-contextual' as Superman, Bob the Builder and the Minions have crept in.

The small number of plays, dramas and narratives offered here are suitable for wide audiences. They belong broadly to the genre of nativity play. As such, they are not dependent on high levels of skill and are very much intended to give scope to actors of all abilities. But they are not intended as sentimental. They attempt to bring out the toughness and lived reality that lies behind our stories of the Christ. Having said that, they are also meant to be fun!

As a preacher and spiritual director I've long been fascinated by sermons and meditations and everything in between. The best sermons and meditations can pack an extraordinary power into relatively few words. They are compelling pointers towards God, but they can also be meeting points with the living God.

In all sorts of ways I know 'the sermon' is dead. We are in the midst of a profoundly visual culture and there's probably not a lot of interest left in the kind of short meditations and reflections contained at the end of the book. However, I still believe that the written word is powerful and there is space and unique value in trying to follow a line of thought in written form. The meditations and sermons presented here are intended as leaping-off points for further reflection and challenges to comfortable patterns of thought.

Perhaps the 'cuckoo in the nest' is the essay entitled 'A Tonka Toy Christmas'. It has appeared in print before, in various forms, firstly in Nicola Slee and Rosie Miles' *Doing December Differently* and then in my theological memoir, *Dazzling Darkness*. Nonetheless, I think it bears repeating. It is a stand-alone piece and a reminder of how challenging Christmas can be for those who don't fit its normative patterns. Nonetheless, I trust it contains a seam of hope which reminds us that Christmas is a feast which is defined, at its deepest, by its divergence from convention. That it is the queerest festival in Christianity.

OH WHAT A NIGHT!

A light-hearted version of the nativity, with serious intent. This can work well with all ages, but depends on skilled and committed delivery. It can be used as a springboard for group discussion about the implications of Nativity in a modern context.

Cast of characters

Joseph – A young man
Mary – A young and very pregnant woman
Stan – A homeless man
Helen – A prostitute
P.J. – Helen's boyfriend. A heroin user.
A crowd of revellers

SCENE 1

Loud music plays.

A GROUP OF REVELLERS stagger into view, perhaps covered in streamers, carrying beer-cans.

They start chanting the name of the local town/city e.g. 'Manchester, Manchester, Manchester …' in a beery fashion, and fall about laughing.

They stagger on a bit, then start singing 'Last Christmas I gave you my heart …' in a suitably drunken manner.

Enter MARY AND JOSEPH.

Joseph carries a suitcase. Both look haggard and harassed, Mary especially.

One of the drunken revellers accidentally bumps into Mary, but seems to ignore her.

Joseph: Oi, watch it! She's pregnant.

The revellers seem to take no notice and move offstage.

Joseph: People today! Just got no manners. *(Joseph 'trawls' his throat, and 'gobs' on the floor.)*

Mary: Oh, forget it. Let's just find somewhere to stay. And, Joseph, will you stop spitting in the street. It's disgusting.

Behind Mary's back, Joseph pulls a face that indicates he feels nagged. He stops when Mary turns to him.

Mary: Look, I think there are some hotels over there. Come on.

Mary and Joseph mime knocking on doors, talking to hoteliers, negotiating a place to stay, constantly being turned away. Mary should become increasingly angry/frustrated; Joe should become more and more despondent/depressed. After a few tries they sit down in the street.

Mary: I just don't believe this. Everywhere's full, and when you ask 'Why?', they just say 'Don't you know it's Christmas?' Whatever that is. I mean, what with that and this damn census we'll never get anywhere. *(Towards Joseph, with real venom)* It's all your fault, this! Why couldn't you have been born somewhere closer to home? But, no, you have to be born a 100 miles from the nearest civilised town ...

Joseph: *(Glumly)* Aw, [local town/city] isn't that bad ...

Mary: And what's worse is we could've got a room if that pathetic car of yours hadn't broken down five miles from town and left us to walk. Huh, car! I say 'car', if that's what you call a 1972 Ford Cortina with furry dice in the window ...

Joseph: It's a classic, that is.

Mary: It's a pile of scrap. When the AA man turned up, he laughed, said, 'I'm not in the comedy business,' and cleared off. And then, to cap it all, here I am like a beached whale ...

Joseph: You said it.

Mary: What?

Joseph: Nothing.

Mary: So here I am ready to pop a sprog at any moment, with only 'Mr Waste of Space 20__' for company. It's about time you *did* something!

Mary puts her head into her hands.

Joseph: (*Directly to the audience*) I know she thinks I'm a fool, but she's no idea how much I love her. Or how scared I am. I just don't know what's going on. I know I'm not the baby's dad, but what am I supposed to do when Mary says the kid's dad is God. What kind of talk is that? I just know I love her and I want to be there for her. And the kid.

Joseph puts his head into his hands.

Mary: *(Directly to the audience)* I know I shouldn't take it out on him, but I'm so scared. He probably thinks I hate him, but if only he knew. I love him. I'm just so confused. I couldn't believe it at first – that God would give me a child. I didn't even want one. I mean, I'm still at school, I want a career. And then I got pregnant. With God's kid! Except no one believed me. But Joseph was there for me. And now we need to find somewhere to stay or this kid's going to be born on the street.

Mary and Joseph look at each other in a loving way, and collapse into each other's arms. At which point Mary goes into labour.

Mary: Oh my God, it's starting. Joseph, it's starting. It's starting! Joseph! DO SOMETHING!!!

Joseph: Right, yes, right! Um … *(Joseph gets up in a fumbling manner; starts running up and down, talking to (imaginary) passers-by, trying to elicit help.)* Look, I wonder if you could … would you? Look, there's a pregnant woman here who needs help … why won't anyone help? HEEELLLPPP!!!!! *(beat)* I know! I'll call an ambulance. *(Joseph fumbles for his mobile phone, but can't find it)* Where's my phone? I can't find my phone. Damn, I bet it's still in the car. *(Joseph mimes talking to 'passers-by' again)* Can I borrow your phone? Please, please … Damn it, why won't anyone help? *(To Mary)* Just wait here. I'll find a pay phone. I'll be back in a minute …

Mary: *(In serious pain)* No, Joseph, no! Don't leave me … I'm scared … ooh, I think it's coming … just get me off the street.

Joseph begins to help Mary to her feet.

Enter STAN

Stan: Here, let me ...

Mary: (*Not fully aware of Stan's presence*) Yeugh, what's that smell?

Joseph: (*Defensively*) I've done nothing!

Stan: Come on, let's get her off the street.

Mary: (*Becoming aware of Stan*) Yeugh, who's this? God, is it a dosser? (*Mary has a new contraction*) Oh no, it's COMING!!

Stan: (*To Joseph*) Look, let's get her off the street. I've got a place down this alley. We'll sort her out from there.

Joseph: Well ...

Stan: We've no time to argue ... Come on!

They help Mary offstage – behind, e.g., a screen. The remaining dialogue in this scene takes place offstage.

Joseph: So where's your place, then?

Stan: This is it.

Joseph: It's a cardboard box and some newspapers.

Stan: It's all I've got.

Mary: (*Shouting in pained anger*) When you two have finished talking about home furnishings, could you get your butts down here and give me a hand. This thing is going to come out any minute …

Joseph: Oh God, I think I'm going to faint …

SCENE 2

The back alley of the previous scene now takes centre stage. There is a cardboard box and papers strewn everywhere. Mary sits, exhausted but happy, against the wall, cradling her baby. (The baby is wrapped in a top/jumper.) Joseph sits next to her, 'coochicooing' over the tot. Stan stands, looking about him.

Stan: *(Almost to himself)* We should get the baby and mother to a hospital.

Joseph overhears this, gets shaken out of his doting, and stands to talk to Stan.

Joseph: Look, I don't know how to thank you … don't even know your name …

Stan: Stan.

Joseph: Er, Joseph … *(They shake hands; then Joseph, visibly losing his reservations, hugs Stan)* And this is my girlfriend … my wife … Mary … Mary, this is Stan …

Mary: Stan, what you did was wonderful … and I'm so sorry about what I said, you know, about you being a dosser …

Stan shrugs.

Mary: Would you like to hold him?

Stan: Erm, no, I don't think I should …

Mary: Please, Stan. I couldn't think of anyone I'd trust more to hold him.

Stan: (*Holding baby*) What are you going to call him?

Mary: (*Looking at Joseph as much as at Stan*) We're going to call him Jesus Emmanuel.

Stan: Cool – a bit weird though …

Mary: It means 'God with us'.

Enter HELEN, a prostitute.

Helen: Hey, Stan, what's happening? You been sowing your wild oats again?

Stan hastily passes the baby back to Mary.

Stan: Oh, Helen, you all right? I'm just helping out this lot.

Helen: So we heard. Your mate Reg saw the whole thing. You're a regular superhero. A few of us were wondering if we could help. Come on Stan, aren't you going to introduce us?

Stan: Yeah, of course, Helen … Mary and Joseph and baby Jesus.

Helen: Cool name – bit weird though.

Stan: Yes, yes, we've done that one already.

Helen crouches down by Mary and Joseph.

Helen: Aw, isn't he gorgeous ... you're so lucky .... look, I know you don't know me, but if you need a nicer place to stay, you can come to mine. It gets a bit hectic, but it's warm.

Stan: *(Sarcastically)* Is that the flat or the bed? Come on Helen, a hooker's flat is hardly the place for a nice family.

Helen: And this is?

Stan: And there's P.J. to deal with.

Helen: Look, he's all right. He'll be here in a minute.

Stan: What do you want to go asking that useless smackhead over for?

Helen: He's just bringing some things for the baby.

Mary: Please, don't argue. You're both great. You've done loads already. But I think it would be wise if Jesus and me went to a hospital to get checked over. What do you think?

Helen: Yeah, you're right.

Joseph: *(Obviously been thinking)* That's it, yes. That's what I was going to do. I'll go and ring for an ambulance.

Stan: I'll come with you if you don't mind.

Joseph: Back in a tick. *(Kisses Mary)*

Helen: You've got a good bloke there.

Mary: He has his uses!

Helen: Look, I brought a few things. I thought you might need them.

Helen takes a blanket out of a carrier bag.

Mary: That's lovely.

Helen: And I found some wipes and a towel – oh and this perfume stuff. If you or baby need to get cleaned up, like. And the smelly stuff is fine for Jesus. It's hypo-allergenic. I checked.

Mary: Thank you. I don't know what to say. We don't deserve all this.

Helen: Don't be silly. It's nothing.

Mary: You're wrong. It's everything … *(beat)*

Joseph and Stan re-enter.

Joseph: All done. The ambulance will be here as soon as it gets through the traffic.

Enter P.J.

Stan: Well, look who it isn't!

P.J.:   Pleasure to see you too, Stan.

Helen: P.J., you got here! Come and meet everyone – Mary, Joseph and the little 'un, Jesus.

P.J.:   Cool name – bit weird though.

Helen: Yes, yes … did you get the things I asked for?

P.J.:   Yeah, nicked 'em from the late-night chemists.

Helen: Oh, P.J.!

P.J.:   Well, old habits and all that. I got nappies and dummies and everything like. I'm a walking maternity ward.

Helen: Well, thanks anyway. *(To Mary)* His heart is in the right place.

Mary: *(To P.J.)* Would you like a look at Jesus?

P.J.:   Oh, could I? Never really been near a baby before. *(Draws in close; start coochicooing, etc.)*

Mary: P.J.'s an unusual name. What does it stand for?

P.J.:   Psycho Jack, but my friends just call me Psycho.

Mary: Lovely ... *(Thinks for a second)* You could hold him if you like.

P.J.:   Aw, could I?

Helen: Now, be careful.

               Stan comes and joins the 'adoration scene'.

Helen: *(To Mary & Joseph)* You two have got someone really special there.

Stan & P.J.:   *(Together)* Yeah!

Mary: It's going to sound stupid, but I think we all have. 'Cos we're all part of his family too ...

               Silence

Stan:	There's some flashing lights. Come on, it's the ambulance. Come on little lad, let's get you in the warm.

EPILOGUE

Stan, Helen and P.J. in line facing the congregation.

Stan:	I never thought I mattered.
Helen:	They called me a tart and a waste of space.
P.J.:	I was labelled a menace to society. Come to think of it, I am a menace to society.
All:	But tonight was different.
Stan:	Because I wasn't ignored.
Helen:	Because I wasn't just being used by someone else.
P.J.:	Because someone let *me* help.
All:	Tonight was different.
Stan:	Tonight I counted.
Helen:	Tonight I was accepted for who I am.
P.J:	Tonight I didn't have to play the thug.
All:	Because of a child Because it was OK to show love

To be vulnerable and real
To see the world in a new way
To be loved
If there is a God, tonight he has been among us.

MAGNIFICAT

A reading suitable for two voices which attempts to place the Magnificat in jux-taposition to the anxiety of teenage pregnancy. It works especially well as a dramatic piece, where the words of the Magnificat are simply read and the other words are 'performed' by a young(-ish) adult. This requires decent acting skills, but is worth the attempt. This piece has been used in a youth-centred context and can act as a springboard for open-ended discussion.

Voice 1:   My soul proclaims the greatness of the Lord,
My spirit rejoices in God my Saviour.

Voice 2:   I'm pregnant.

Voice 1:   For you, Lord, have looked with favour on your lowly servant.

Voice 2:   I'm 14 and I'm pregnant.

Voice 1:   You, the Almighty, have done great things for me
And holy is your name.

Voice 2:   Mum'll kill me.

Voice 1:   You have mercy on those who fear you,
From generation to generation.

Voice 2:   I'll get rid of it. Before it shows. She'll never know.

Voice 1:   You have shown strength with your arm
And scattered the proud in their conceit.

Voice 2:   I'll know.

Voice 1:   Casting down the mighty from their thrones
And lifting up the lowly.

Voice 2:   Help me. Please help me.

Voice 1:   You have filled the hungry with good things
And sent the rich away empty.

Voice 2:   It's not fair.

Voice 1:   You have come to the aid of your servant Israel
To remember the promise of mercy.

Voice 2:   It's just not fair.

Voice 1:   The promise made to our forebears,
To Abraham and his children for ever.

Voice 2:   I'm 14 and I'm pregnant.

YET ANOTHER MOUTH TO FEED

This is a drama that can be fully staged or partially staged, but may be adapted for 'dramatic' reading. It attempts to take the nativity and place it in a suburban or urban modern setting.

Cast

Narrator

Farida, a young mum

Voice 1/Passer-by

Voice 2

Voice 3

Voice 4

Narrator: The street was asleep …

FARIDA – behind screen/offstage – makes sounds we might connect with a person giving birth

Narrator: (*Looks puzzled/clears throat*) The street was asleep …

Farida continues to make birth sounds and waddles onstage, visibly very pregnant.

Voice 1:   (*Offstage*) WILL YOU PLEASE SHUT UP!!!

Narrator: (*To Farida. Losing his rag, but remaining very polite*) I say, would you mind being quiet? I'm trying to introduce a story …

Farida: (*Through gritted teeth*) I can't … I'm having a baby, you idiot (*She screams/moans again*)

Narrator: Oh … right … I see … you see, it's your story I'm trying to tell … you couldn't just hold on a minute while I introduce you properly?

Farida: *(Mimicking N's voice)* Hold on a minute?? *(With venom)* JUST GET ME SOME HELP, NOWWWWWW!!

Narrator: Erm, yes, I say, is there anyone who can help?

Farida sits down uncomfortably.

Voice 2:   *(Offstage/sleepily)* Oi – get your skates on – I think Farida's come early.

Voice 3:   So what? Go back to sleep.

Voice 2:   *(Alert now)* Get some towels and hot water. NOW!!

Voice 4:   What the bloody hell's going on?

Voice 2:   It's Farida. She's come early …

Voice 4:   Bloody hell. I'll get me coat …

VOICES 2, 3, 4 appear and begin to collect and gather various items around FARIDA – e.g. water bowl, towels, etc. Someone gets a camera/phone, someone else picks up a present.

FARIDA – surrounded by neighbours – 'has' a baby.

The scene ends with a lovely TABLEAU of mother with child, neighbours surrounding her, offering presents, and someone from the congregation taking a happy picture.

Passer-by: (*Gesturing towards tableau*) How sweet! But it'll never last. How could it? It's just another baby, just another mouth to feed. It's not as if she's special, is it?

Voice 2: Well, no.

Voice 3: Well, maybe.

Voice 4: Well, yes. Every baby's special isn't it?

All: (*Except Passer-by*) Yeah!!

Farida: It's the best thing I've ever done!

Passer-by: Yeah, yeah. But it's not SPECIAL is it?

Voice 2: So what? So what if Farida isn't [name of celebrity]? So what if this isn't [posh place]? What's wrong with being just another baby? Ok, this isn't the nicest street in the world – people have got it tough – but at least we're not stuck up, mate.

Passer-by: But this place is a pit. It's just not right to bring a kid into it.

Voice 3: Listen to [Lady/Lord] Muck here! Alright […] isn't perfect. But I tell you – something special's happened. I've got a god-daughter for a start.

Voice 4: And that rushed job in the night brought out half the street.

Voice 2: And we sorted Farida's husband out with a drop of the hard stuff to calm his nerves. Not that he drunk it, mind, on account of his faith …

Voice 3:   And there's been a whip round for some new paint for the bedroom.

Voice 4:   And the kids all want to play with the new baby …

Passer-by: Oh, please God! Spare me! You'll be talking about the Dunkirk spirit next!

Voice 3:   Well, stuff you too … listen, mate, maybe you're right – maybe all this good will won't last … maybe in a few days everyone'll be beating hell out of each other … but I'll take what I can when I can … and if a baby can teach us that caring for each other is better than fighting, I'll take a risk on that.

A PICTURE OF HOPE

In the popular mind, 'hope' can be very difficult to distinguish from 'optimism'. However, whenever I try to picture 'hope' my mind turns to specifics. For it's not about some vague belief that tomorrow will be better than today. For me, nothing quite demonstrates the concrete and embodied nature of hope than one particular story.

In the aftermath of the Great War, a group of Quakers travelled to Poland to help with the reconstruction of a country and community broken by four years of war and disease. Villages were practically wiped out because of Spanish influenza and cholera. But the Quakers were fearless. In the village where they served, they tended the cholera victims with patience, care and solicitude, using that language of love which transcends our normal vulgar means of communication. But, loving though they were, the Quakers were not superhuman. They fell victim to cholera and died.

The surviving villagers had grown to love these kind and gentle people. They looked on them as strangers who had become their friends. Because they weren't Catholics the parish priest said that the Quakers could not be buried on holy ground. With regret, he insisted that they be buried in a little plot just outside the edge of the churchyard.

Yet, as the village rose from its slumbers on the day after the funerals, a remarkable sight greeted them: in the night the fence of the graveyard had been moved so that the Quakers' graves were inside rather than out.

I've no idea if the events recounted in this story happened quite as described. I'm not sure it really matters. This story – rather like one of Jesus' parables – is truth-bearing and truth-shaping. It draws us closer to our vocation to love, serve and be remade in each other. This story presents a lived and enacted hope.

It is stating the obvious – that we live in a dangerous and violent world. There are countless natural and human crises and disasters. Our vanity and greed condemn generations to war and perdition. The truth is – almost certainly – that it has always been thus. Jesus' time was a riven time. His death is an icon of not only human but state-legislated violence against the living body.

It can feel difficult to figure out what 'hope' looks like, in the modern age as at any point in history. But I always return to the simple human story of people motivated by their faith to serve, and who – in doing so – break down barriers of mistrust and fear. Hope is not some vague optimism that the future will be better. Hope is building community based on seeing the human in people we might fear, or see as strange or even dangerous. It is not giving up, even when it might cost us our lives.

ADVENT AS PREPARATION

When I was twenty-one I went to work as a teacher in a school in Jamaica. In all honesty, before I went it felt like a dream come true. Like many people growing up in the '70s and '80s I'd been exposed to a lot of reggae. Quite apart from the well-known grooves of Bob Marley, I loved the music of Burning Spear, Bunny Wailer, Sly and Robbie and so on. I was – at that time – also a fan of marijuana. From a distance, going to Jamaica looked like a win on every level: I had the promise of a job, I was going to be close to the world of reggae, there would be ganja in abundance and I'd be living on a tropical island.

Nonetheless, I was aware enough to know that moving to Jamaica would be a shock. Jamaica was – as those of us in the privileged 'first world' then said – a 'third-world' country. It was also a former British colony marked by imperial abuses and a history of slavery and white privilege. Before going I spent weeks reading up on the culture of the island. I did everything I could to get beyond the stereotypes of Jamaica as a tropical paradise. In short, I decided that if I was going to get my head around another culture, 'preparation' seriously mattered.

But the moment I landed in Kingston, I freaked out. I knew it was going to be hot, but I found the heat relentless. I knew people spoke a different language, Patois, but I was disoriented for months. Patois was especially frustrating because it shares many words and sounds with English and Jamaican English. I was constantly on the edge of understanding, yet unable to tune in. For the first time in my life I felt stupid and slow and marginalised.

I knew that there were major economic and social issues but I was shocked by the levels of poverty, homophobia and violence. I will never quite recover from seeing people with complex mental health issues simply abandoned to their fate in Kingston because the state could not afford to support and care for them as they deserved.

At the same time, no book or song could have prepared me for the staggering generosity of people with absolutely nothing or the talent of musicians or the startling beauty of mangrove swamps, beaches and hills.

Was I wrong to try and prepare for this adventure? I don't think so. In any important human experience, preparation helps us orient ourselves to the challenges we face. When I've had major surgery or taken exams or lived halfway around the world, being prepared has helped me adapt to new and often exciting challenges and possibilities.

This is one reason why Christians treat Advent, the season in the run up to Christmas, as a time of preparation. We try to spend extra time in prayer and reflection, even fasting, ahead of celebrating the birth of Jesus. And – just as with my experience of going to Jamaica – in one sense no amount of preparation can ready me for the joy of celebrating Jesus' birth on Christmas Day. But I do it anyway – because preparation signals how important the event is. Parents tell me you can never prepare for the shock of holding that new bundle of joy in your arms. But you try anyway, because that new child is worthy of it.

LIGHT IN THE DARKNESS

About fifteen years ago I was persuaded to go into the Blue John Cavern in the Peak District. Ok, it was in the larger, easy to access bit, but I was still nervous. I'd never been in a huge underground cave before. I've never understood the appeal of caving. The thought of being under the ground in a confined space where a few lamps might be all that keeps you from total darkness is not appealing. If I'm entirely honest, my picture of going into caves was drawn from the '80s espionage classic *Edge of Darkness*, in which the protagonist ends up in a cavern full of nuclear waste and receives a massive dose of radiation poisoning.

Despite all of this psychological baggage, I actually enjoyed going underground. Thankfully it seemed quite civilised – we didn't have to crawl through holes and the lighting was bright and impressive. Indeed, it was all going well until, half an hour in, our guide turned all the lights out. It was my first experience of what I can only call 'absolute darkness'.

To this day I still recall feeling my pupils trying to adjust to the darkness, straining for even a hint of light. And not finding any. My eyes were open, but I could not see. At that moment I was desperate for the tiniest bit of light in the darkness. But there was none to be found.

Before the advent of electricity, when there was little light pollution, perhaps it was easier to understand why Jesus was called the Light of the World. Our culture tends to associate darkness with negativity and nastiness and light with goodness, purity and holiness. God as the light helping people to see their way in dark and dangerous times is a powerful idea in a world where winter nights would have been very dark indeed.

I often wonder if both religion and culture are too obsessed with light as positive and darkness as negative. Indeed, my experience of reading Black and Womanist theology, amongst many other things, has revealed Western culture's racist and ruthless obsession with treating 'blackness', 'darkness' and, indeed, anything 'non-white' as tainted, the lesser and the other. The work of a blind theologian like John Hull reminds us that biblical and theological obsessions with light are ableist and in constant danger of excluding the positive life experiences of unsighted people.

The poet Henry Vaughan once wrote, 'There is in God … a deep but dazzling darkness.' One of the things I've heard people say he means is that there is no place where God's light cannot reach, even into the deepest darkness. But I think he's saying something more interesting. That God isn't pure light. Because sometimes too much light is polluting. I only realised this the first time I saw the Milky Way in all its wonder. I was on a small boat in the Caribbean off Jamaica, far from the lights of the shore. If I hadn't been shrouded in darkness I would not have seen one of the most beautiful sights in the universe. Darkness isn't always negative. Sometimes the Dark opens our eyes to see the most amazing things.

ON HATING CHRISTMAS

Making confessions makes us feel better. Apparently it is one of the terrible truths of the 'practice' of interrogation and torture that, even if the accused is innocent, they will – at the end of the interrogation – feel 'relief' in making a confession.

My small confession is that I can't bear Christmas. Before you write to the authorities suggesting I be 'unfrocked' for not believing in the birth of Jesus, let me explain. It's not the birth of a child two thousand years ago in Palestine I struggle with; it's the way Christmas has become a festival of excess wrapped up in gloopy sentimentality.

Don't get me wrong, I love an excuse to party with family and friends and exchange gifts of love. But I despair at the way the extraordinary story of Jesus' birth has been trumped by a competition about who has the most ridiculous Christmas jumper or has spent the most on presents.

The Bible's accounts of Jesus' birth are very far from being sweet and sentimental. They paint a picture of a child whose birth is so unprivileged that he's born in a stable and whose first cot is an animal's feeding trough. His parents have been forced to leave their home town by oppressive authorities and they later have to flee and become refugees in Egypt.

One of the titles Christians give to Jesus is 'God-with-us'. But the Bible gives a shocking picture of this God-with-us. Jesus is not the God of power and glory, but a God who – in coming to us as a baby – is utterly dependent upon us for his survival. This is the Christmas that speaks to me. For in focusing on God coming to be with us as a vulnerable baby, Christmas shows us the kind of love we're invited to embody – not a half-hearted love that says, 'I'll be generous to you as long as you give me something in return,' but a love that's based on extravagant generosity. That is based on being alongside God in the weakest and most vulnerable and those least able to repay us for our love.

DOWN IN THE OLD WOOD

Down in the old wood, the heartwood, of our selves is a place – a kind of grove – filled with wild and twisted trees. Strange fruit grow there, and peculiar music is heard. It can be a difficult place to get to and many ask why you would want to go there anyway: better, they say, to stay in the newer forests of the self, among the saplings, where there is clearly new life and light, where there is space to breathe and the songs are familiar and everyday. But right down in each of us is a sacred grove, and its music is ancient and troubling. Some pray and some fast for years to get there, to the spring of our being. Others just shy away. It is a place where the Spirit would make us and unmake us, and its music is blue as a corpse, red as a fresh-cut artery. The prophets have always sung these deepest songs, and musicians often arrive unexpectedly in the sacred grove only to discover they are home. And they would take us there, these singers of God's love, to the heartwood of our selves, where this grove is waiting for us to know it as home and be transformed by the Spirit which longs to sing within us too.

> Spirit of God,
> enable us to be unafraid
> of the deepest music, of your sacred songs;
> may we dance with the prophets
> to your homecoming tune.
> Amen

CHRISTMAS – WHERE IS IT HAPPENING?

Life often feels like it's happening elsewhere, to other, more interesting people. In the past week I've had a number of conversations which have underlined this.

For the sake of protecting confidentiality, it is obviously unfair to mention names and too many details. But those conversations have shared an important characteristic – a sense of 'life not really happening for/to me'; a feeling of being a bit neglected and left out of the action, of not quite 'being seen'.

It's an experience that is most common among people who (on the face of it) lack the means to shape their own lives – the housebound, for example, who experience marginalisation and feel they lack power, authority and the means to shape conditions of respect around them.

I remember when I was really ill, years ago now, and I relied on benefits to support me. I was a highly educated and, in some ways, confident person, but the experience corroded my sense of place and worth. (I hate to think just how awful 'life beneath the line' is for people dealing with our current vile benefits regime. Indeed, in our divided society, work itself is no longer, in many cases, the means to lift oneself to a place of dignity.)

However, I suspect feeling 'unseen' or 'at the edges' is an experience all of us have from time to time – even the rich and powerful. Let's leave aside whether that's justified. My point is that one can so easily get caught up in one's context and not see it for what it is.

I also think that social media amplify this experience. It is so very easy, via Twitter or Facebook, to catch a glimpse of other people's lives. Given that these glimpses are so often carefully curated insights into the 'best' or 'most exciting' parts of those lives, it can leave us feeling inadequate.

I am not someone who has many grounds for self-pity or for believing that 'the real action is elsewhere'. I have one hell of a rich and creative life. But I'm as bad as anyone else for feeling left out. I suspect that reflects one of the flaws in my personality – I love to feel like 'an insider'. For example, I'm one of those people who, when I go to the theatre, really wants to be in the show. I don't need to be on stage (no matter what my younger brother says!), just to be on the inside.

I'm not particularly proud of this trait, but it's worth acknowledging it. It can mean that even if things are varied and fun in my life, I might look at other people and think, 'Well, they're having more fun' or 'getting to do cool things' or 'living a more interesting or more influential life' and so on. It's all rather tedious, but real nonetheless.

It's rather like the story of the Jesuit novice who envied a colleague because the latter was clearly ace at prayer and silence and contemplation. Finally the novice told the 'expert' contemplative how much he envied him. To which the contemplative replied how much he envied the novice back. Why? Because the novice was so committed to social action and engagement and the contemplative wished he found it as easy to be with people. So often 'the world', 'the action' and 'the life' can seem to be going on in other people's glamorous or powerful or busy or, frankly, different lives.

This phenomenon is one reason we all need Christmas. For the 'power' of Christmas – as symbol, story, narrative, myth (I really don't care if the first nativity happened 'exactly' like the Gospel record) – lies in its reminder of the Divine's/God's disinterest in glamour, cool and position. It reminds us that God, as ultimate Other, does not need all the things many of us think are fundamental, but are actually props for our vanity or position.

Where is Christmas happening? Clearly, the easy answer is everywhere. Everywhere the tinsel goes up, and there are songs of good cheer and so on.

Those of us who are religious need to remember that we don't 'own' Christmas. Or perhaps Christmas happens among those who believe in the Christ, who gather to share his story and are united in belief and liturgy. It's not my job to put limits on where Christmas can and does happen.

However, the Bible narratives offer some powerful suggestions that undercut many of our easy assumptions. Christmas substantially undermines our vainglorious pictures of what is important and significant in the world and our lives.

Jesus Christ – as icon of God – is not born in a temple or palace, among kings and emperors and hierophants. He is not born at the heart of a metropolis or political centre. His place of birth is no Rome or Jerusalem, but a no-note town that barely retains the rumours of a once-great king. There is no glamour or cool, just a stable and peasants for parents. One of the parents isn't even – on some readings of the biblical text – the 'birth' parent.

The eyes of the world are not upon Jesus; there are no reporters waiting at the door for a quote from the proud mum or dad. There are just shepherds. Not the romantic figures of Victorian sentiment, but unrighteous men and women who plied their trade in lonely hills far away from the rituals that might make them pure and upright.

This icon of God – Jesus – was, as the song has it, 'a saviour without safety', without any means of self-defence, except for the effects that a baby can have on stony hearts. He was placed into the hands of humans as adequate and inadequate as any of us. He was dependent, open to abuse and neglect, and yet calling forth love.

We live in an age of carefully curated lives, where so many of us calculate how best we can make an impact, get ahead, ensure our voices are heard. And, damn it, some voices should be heard, though probably not the ones who get the most 'airtime'.

We live in an age of shiny things, where – understandably – even as Christians we want to be seen in the market place and public square. (And I'm clear that faith voices have much to contribute beyond safe 'holy huddles'.)

We live in an age where it can feel like all that is good is happening in the palaces and modern temples of money and glamour and power. And anyone may feel left out or unseen.

But I sense God is about other things.

Where is Christmas happening this year? Probably in some neglected, uncomfortable part of the estate on which you (or should I say 'I') live, without much attention or seeming value. Right there, good news will be happening, a commitment to love and act for the good by people who seem to be nobodies to those whose attention is fixed elsewhere.

Where is Christmas happening this year? Perhaps in the passion and pain, but unconquerable courage, of LGBT people in Africa, whose voices are as marginalised as Christ's, who are being made to bleed without safety and justice.

Where is Christmas happening this year? Among those whom this society and others treat as unrighteous, as outcasts, and as the nobodies who are told never to expect glory or wonder or joy. Perhaps Christmas is happening among those seeking refuge and asylum and among those taking the risk of granting it. Perhaps.

Perhaps we cannot quite say, under the conditions our society finds itself living through, where Christmas will be happening.

However, the Nativity is a reminder that if Christmas – or life or whatever – is happening 'elsewhere', it is not in the 'elsewhere' of glamorous, powerful and influential lives.

Christmas is not in the homes of those who insulate themselves from terror, pain and exposure to reality, who create simulacra of Christmas for the benefit of telling themselves they are the special or honoured ones.

The elsewhere of Christmas is all around us, in the world we choose not to see, that won't be dressed up in an ironic Christmas jumper and made to look festive. And in that otherness God is alive and seen by those with eyes to see. And from those places God comes to tear down the palaces and the temples of our easy comfort and exploitation. God's star points us not towards glitz or status, but into a more fearful glory.

O THAT YOU WOULD TEAR OPEN THE HEAVENS

'O that you would tear open the heavens and come down,
So that the mountains would quake at your presence'

What a world we live in! We have technological wonder, we have medical treatments undreamt of thirty years ago, and people are living ever longer – yet so many things never seem to change. Are there really any fewer poor people in the world today? Is there any less fear? There are always the doom-sayers and Cassandras who want to convince us that the end of the world is just around the corner, but so many people I know are genuinely and real-istically fearful for their jobs, or for the future of the planet and the way in which we are inclined to treat it to suit our convenience. We who live com-fortable lives can barely begin to comprehend how the other 95% of the world live. And why is there such little justice for good people? Why so much undeserved suffering?

I know of no caring person of faith who has not – in some form or another – cried out to God like Isaiah: 'O that you would tear open the heavens and come down, so that the mountains would quake at your presence.' That is, who has not wished that the Lord God Almighty would reach down and sort out the mess. It is one of the deepest desires of the human, praying heart. It is the desire for hope and justification. It is the hope that the humiliations of the poor and the oppressed and the despised will be vindicated in one bound.

During Advent we are called to do at least two things: get ready to receive the Christ Child into our lives once again, and look forward to what is often called the 'Second Coming' – the consummation of everything, the new heaven and the new earth.

How can we hear Isaiah's words in a world of need?

Surely we are right to be hungry for God's presence and God's vindication. To be hungry for God's justice must be right and of God. And yet … and yet … who is this God that we are hungry for?

When we want God to come down and show his arm, his presence, his power, I suspect that often what we're after is a kind of superhero God. A Superman who will make all the pain and fear and worry go away. In the classic cartoon *The Simpsons*, after yet another problem emerges in his life, the immortal everyman and father-figure Homer exclaims, 'I'm not normally a religious man ... but if you're up there, Superman, I could sure use your help.'

This at least would be an obviously useful God – a God we could all understand, religious or not. This God would come and sort out our scrapes, make sure that fewer people were killed in tragic accidents, and properly punish bad deeds.

Secretly there are times when we all want that God, I think.

Yet this is not how God comes to dwell with us. God joins us as a baby – without glamour, without status, with minimal shelter and under conditions of real threat. We should not lose sight of the implications of this.

Babies are, frankly, at various times, smelly, crying and extraordinarily needy things. And dare I say it – you're going to hate me for this – they're not very interesting. They really don't do very much: they gurgle, sleep, cry, poo and wee, sleep some more, and stare into space.

And yet they are extraordinary. And not just because we know what they may become – strong, dynamic, exciting adults who will take humankind on into the next generation and open up new worlds for us. Their amazing power lies in themselves. In the miracle of life they represent. Their value is not predicated on whether they're able or will ever be able to do x, y or z. They remind us of the fundamental dignity of humans – regardless of ability and so on.

Any person, religious or unreligious, gives thanks when their child has been safely delivered and this is because babies come to us as gifts. They are ours and yet we know that they are not ours. We hold them for a time but in the end love demands that we let them go and be their own selves.

And so God comes to us not as a superhero, but as a baby. This is not what we want, but it is actually what we need. For babies remind us of our responsibilities and they call us out of ourselves. They bring us into relationship – a relationship based on serious and profound love.

There's a big problem with the superhero God – 'he' expects nothing of us. We get into trouble and he saves us. We are like little children. There's a problem in the world and he comes and sorts it. And yes, each of us can reasonably think that we could do with a little more help from time to time and I certainly don't want any of us to believe we're on our own – we are part of a great fellowship of faith bound by the Spirit – but God is inviting us to step out of childish pictures of God and become who we might be.

And thus – the baby. Sent in love as a gift to invite us to lavish our love. To give our praise and thanksgiving and also to act and be more than we imagine we can be.

We have within us a capacity for extraordinary, committed love – not just for our own children and families and friends, but for a world groaning for hope and salvation.

The arrival of God among us is more than just an opportunity for a warm, glowing celebration; it is an invitation to step up and become people of great love, committed to justice. As we get ready to meet the Christ Child again, let us prepare our hearts and minds to leap out beyond our settled, comfortable ways and lavish love on a fearsomely needy world.

A WORLD OF DISTRACTION –
HEARING GOD IN THE SOUND OF PURE SILENCE

Last time I counted, I had around 250 to 300 TV channels on my cable service. And if you want a classic example of what an easily distracted, easily bored mind looks like, come and see me on a Saturday or Sunday afternoon – just after lunch – flicking through those channels. How often have I said to myself, 'There's nothing on,' and proceeded to flick through every one of the channels, one after the other? Sometimes I stop briefly, but inevitably pass on to the next until I've done the full tour. And you know the best bit? By the time I've got through all 300, I've forgotten what was on the first one and I can start all over again. I've wasted whole days just clicking 'the clicker', as my mum calls it. Click, click, click.

During Advent – that great time of preparation and waiting – I wonder whether the great modern sin or symbol of 'brokenness' and alienation is Distraction. I worry that we are in danger of becoming human versions of 'Dory', the character from *Saving Nemo*: attention span nil. Or do we risk becoming human magpies – forever chasing after 'shiny things'? 'Ooh, look at that shiny, shiny thing,' we say. Whether that be a new phone, or new boots or a new gadget. And I know some of us will be thinking, 'Well I'm too old/too clever to be caught up in that sort of trendy thing.' But let's not forget that we are all the objects of advertising and marketing. Many of us have settled tastes and views, but there is always something about to appear on the TV to tempt us, whether a new cereal, a new car or some super cleaning product.

It's often said that modern living is very fast. With Facebook, Twitter, instant messaging and so on people have never been able to communicate and connect more quickly. Everything gets abbreviated to boot. But as much as I love all that stuff, the danger is that we are in such a dash to get things done that we lack consideration and generosity. We are especially under pressure at this time of the year – making ready for Christmas and all that surrounds it. I trust that what we do is good and rewarding, but do we really prepare in the way God wants us to, the way God is inviting us to?

What does real preparation look like? When we get ready for a big event we usually make sure we've got food and drink in, set up the venue, put our glad rags on, and so on and so forth. But God isn't interested in fantastic spreads and party frocks. She is inviting us deeper and elsewhere. God wants us to get ready to meet her once again in the shape of the Christ Child – to allow her to fill and inspire our imaginations. And getting ready to receive is demanding and exciting in quite different ways from what we often end up doing during Advent.

This preparation for Christ invites us to do something counter-intuitive. At a time of great pressure, of parties, of a sense of gathering momentum, God invites us to do one simple thing: to stop and breathe and be still. Why is that so hard? Maybe it's because we're afraid of silence; or maybe it's because we're sick to death of silence. I've heard many people who live on their own say, 'I can't bear all that quiet. That's why I have the radio on or make sure I'm very busy.' Maybe it's because we've got so much on or we live in a busy house. But surely that makes stillness and silence even more important.

Sometimes people say, 'I'm too busy to pray,' but surely it should be, 'I'm too busy not to pray.' And by prayer here I mean taking time with God; I mean settling down to be with God as one might settle down to read a good book or watch a transporting drama or film. It can mean a quiet day alone or spending time with a prayer group. Stillness and silence matter so much because God doesn't have a shouty, hectoring voice. Our God is a God of invitation, of kindness, who respects our free will. She doesn't force herself on us like an unctuous relative. She isn't like a heavy-handed salesperson who rings us up and tries to sell us something. God waits on us to call and in stillness we might hear her voice.

In the book of Kings, we hear that famous story of Elijah going to the mountain, an incident described in the hymn 'Dear Lord and Father of Mankind'. He listens for God in the thunder and the lightning, then in the wind and the earthquake, and finally hears God in the 'still small voice of calm'. My favourite translation of the Hebrew is 'hearing God in the sound of pure silence'. Pure silence. Well, if you live in a big city, like I do, you're going to struggle to find pure silence. There are probably only a couple of places in the world where you can get that. But please, if you do nothing else in the run up to Christmas, take some time out with God. Know that you are her beloved child. Be prepared to receive the joyous news of her Child once again.

And if that seems too easy and comfortable, consider this. Stillness and silence are no mere prompt for some sort of cosy, self-centred 'mindfulness', an individual sense of place and location (no matter how important that might be). They are the prompt for clearing away the clutter of distraction so that we – as community – can focus on God's vocation to justice and mercy and peace. It is a stripping away of the distractions which lead us to seek after secondary things rather than seeing that God comes that we might have life and have it abundantly. And that abundant life, it seems to me, is not based on owning all the consumer toys we could ever want to tell us we're successful, loved and special. That abundant life is exposure – to others, to others' needs, to their love – which draws us out of our individual bunkers to meet with our fellow humans on fragile and common ground.

EMPTINESS

I read of a man in the USA who suffers from a rare and frankly dreadful disease which means he can never, ever feel full up. No matter how much he eats he still feels hungry and his body tells him he needs more. Imagine how awful it must be to experience a constant sense of emptiness in one's stomach. We've all known that feeling at some time, and some of us perhaps know what it is really to go hungry. But this man has that feeling all the time. He eats and eats and is never full. And of course he is overweight and a focus of ridicule in a world where being fat is treated as a reason for making jokes. People don't understand that he can't just choose not to eat. I don't know if there's any treatment, but I do know that that man is in a terrible situation.

Advent strikes me as good time to reflect on 'hunger'. For I fear the problem our world, our society and many of us as individuals are dealing with in a consumerist culture, especially as Christmas approaches, is a sense of raging emptiness. I suspect that the challenge we face goes something like this: sometime within the last forty years or so, the people in the rich countries stopped being regarded as citizens and were relabelled as 'consumers'. We are no longer producers of goods or resources; we just consume. The Latin root of the word we use has implications of both eating and wasting. For us, everything is about consumption – not just food, but goods and services, even education. We live in a world where banks call the services they offer 'products' which we are then invited to consume. Though, frankly, the cynic within me fails to see how a loan is a product – a product is surely something we can touch and hold.

In a consumerist world, the most important thing is to keep consuming. It's what keeps the economy on track. In other words, what's important is that we are kept hungry for more and more stuff. Reductions on consumer taxes like VAT are designed not to give us more money in our pockets but to whet our appetite to spend. I'm not saying anything new when I say we live in a society that relies more on spending than producing. But the implication, I want to say, is that we become as individuals and as a society ever more like that man who is never full. My question is: when is enough enough?

It's a question I ask myself all the time – but it can't just be an issue for me. I fill my life and house with stuff, the latest gadgets, endless food, and I can't see that they satisfy. I have so much food in my house I often have to throw piles of it away because I never eat it in time. I worry that so many of us are trying to sate our endless hunger for more, and that crucially this hunger is really a hunger for meaning, and the things we choose to try to feed it with don't satisfy. It's like eating junk food – we want it, we seek it out, we eat it quickly, but then it's gone and we are just as hungry. And the worst of it is that we live in a culture which seems to rely on our always wanting more and getting more and never being filled. Perhaps John the Baptist was right in living off wild honey and locusts – I guess at the very least he'd do well in the bush tucker trial in *I'm a Celebrity, Get Me Out of Here.*

Please don't get me wrong – I'm not being a killjoy. I love feasting; I love partying. I love to celebrate. And, unlike John the Baptist, Jesus himself enjoyed eating and drinking with others; loved to be at the party. But at a deeper level, if all this stuff that we so often want and hunger after can't satisfy, what will? What is the real food we should be seeking? What feeds us not only with enough but with abundance?

I think you can probably guess my answer. Jesus says, 'I am the bread of life and whoever comes to me will never be hungry.' This is a reminder of why sharing our sacred meal – our Eucharist – is so important. To be hungry for Christ – for his peace, his love, his compassion, his generosity – is, I suspect, the deepest human hunger. It is at the heart of our search for meaning in a confusing and troubling world. Buying things gives us a moment's thrill, eating a fine meal satisfies for a while, but it is Christ who is our true peace. And we do not know our rest until we know our rest in God.

Jesus also says, 'Blessèd are you who are hungry now, for you will be filled.' Even among the privileged countries of the North, physical hunger has become a daily reality for many. Wealthy societies are increasingly ordering their peoples' needs and the wider social economy around 'food banks'. They seem to be a strategy of a neo-liberal capitalist economic regime. Given that reality and the fact that 'hunger' is a defining characteristic of life for hundreds of millions of people in the majority world, there should be no rush to spiritualise Jesus' words. When we talk about hunger, if we are not being concrete and 'this-worldly' then we are betraying God's definitive commitment to the world.

But it is, of course, possible to be hungry for 'righteousness'. I think a lot of tosh gets spoken about this concept. As if it is most clearly understood in a context where personal morality – around sex especially – is at stake. Righteousness is, I suspect, about wanting a world which is filled with ever more love and where people trust ever more in God as shown in Jesus Christ. And that hunger is very much a hunger for change in this world. If the gospel doesn't change us, doesn't help us to be bread for others, it's not good news. We are not called to be a holy huddle or a club of like-minded people; we are called to hunger for God and to help others be fed by the God they are seeking. How will you, this week, help others – not just friends but colleagues, acquaintances, even strangers – to draw closer to the Living Bread of Christ?

IN THE WILDERNESS

I'd like you to close your eyes for a moment and imagine your dream holiday – you know, the kind of place where you'd like to be if money were no object. Imagine that place in as much detail as you can.

I suspect not many readers would visualise a trip to the middle of the Sahara desert. A number of us might fancy visiting the pyramids in Egypt, but very, very few people would want to go on holiday to the heart of a desert – to the proverbial sea of sand. It is a lonely, fierce and dangerous place, where temperatures can easily top 100 degrees F during the day and plummet to below freezing at night. It is nothing more or less than a total wilderness. Even after watching something like Michael Palin's *Sahara*, few of us imagine how vast and featureless a desert can be. The idea of it being a 'dream destination' is surely absurd. Lots of us want sea and sand, but we'd be furious if our holiday company dumped us in the middle of a metaphorical sea of sand.

I want to talk about thirst. And where better to go to talk about that than the desert? I grew up watching Sunday afternoon war films – things like *Ice Cold in Alex* and *Sea of Sand*. These tales of the Desert War in World War Two always featured scenes of sweating soldiers labouring over sand dunes, desperate with thirst, searching for the next oasis, seeing mirages. If you want to know about thirst, go and spend some time in a desert.

I sense that the deeper we journey into God, the closer we get to know her, the more God invites us to make the desert, the wilderness, our home. That is, the closer we draw to God, the thirstier we might become because the drier the road becomes. I want to try to give some account of this experience of being drawn deeper into God. I'm not going to pretend that it's easy to understand. But if we're serious about growing as Christians I think we need to wrestle with it.

What most of us want out of life is, well, a pretty good time. We'd like to be popular, or wealthy, or blessed with a loving family, whether that be our church or our natural family. We'd like to be comfortable; maybe with one or two challenges to liven things up, but nothing we can't stand. That's the kind of thing I sense I want. Nobody, but nobody, unless they're verging on the masochistic, wants a life of misery or hardship. (To put it another way, nobody with sense wants to end up in the middle of the desert with little to sustain them. Only the exceptionally holy or crazy, or both, would choose it.)

Now, when it comes to our relationship with God perhaps something similar takes place. Perhaps what we want from our relationship with God is something reasonably comfortable; with one or two challenges, but with nothing that is really hard work. God is maybe like an idealised parent or sibling or friend – someone we can talk to, if we're lucky, but who doesn't poke their nose too deeply into our business. We go to God when we need help or direction, but otherwise we're happier if she doesn't move into our house and try to organise our life.

And even for those of us who want to get to know God better, perhaps what we hope for is that as we learn to pray more deeply, or listen to God more attentively or be more faithful to her Word, things will just keep getting better and better. For surely if we're faithful to God she will bless us with more and more good things, won't she? Our prayer will grow ever richer; our joy in the Lord will only increase and so on. If we are good children we'll get good things. If it's what we expect from a human parent, shouldn't it be more so with God, the ultimate parent?

Well, it's an appealing fantasy, and there are a good number of churches out there that are inclined to suggest it. I have this hunch that God is faithful to us in quite different ways; that when we go deeper with God we are led not into some great garden of earthly delights where everything gets easier and easier, but out into the desert. That she gives us only a greater thirst for her Kingdom. I suspect the God of Jesus and the Israelites is a God of the wilderness and the desert. She leads her faithful children out into the purifying dryness of the wilderness to be prepared for new things. To ready our thirst for the full coming of the Kingdom. And I find this strangely encouraging. The fact is that most of us feel like life is a pretty tough, thirsty place with only a few oases to sustain our spirit. But this is the place of preparation and discovery. Even Jesus himself had to walk in the desert and face temptation. Ironically, the harsh places are the places where we discover most about ourselves and who we are in God. We would not choose them; I'm not even sure God wants them for us; but they are, in the end, unavoidable if we are to be who God is calling us to be. God leads us into the desert to speak into our hearts without the distractions with which we fill our lives.

Maybe there are only a few of us who ever truly come to love the desert; but each of us must be unafraid to travel there. For as God's pilgrim people our only hope of finding the promised land lies across the wilderness. Before we arrive at Bethlehem with Mary and Joseph, the shepherds and the Magi there are journeys to be undertaken. But when we come to gaze in wonder on the Christ Child, we shall know true peace and joy.

LIVING ON PROMISES

Isaiah 11:1-10

I use buses a lot. I know they're not to everyone's taste, but they're fabulous ways of conveying lots of people from place to place, and newer buses are becoming more environmentally friendly all the time. I suspect no one enjoys buses at commute time however. Before I was ordained I often travelled to work by bus and hated it. Surely no one thinks – as they get up on a work day morning - 'Yippee! I've got to get the bus again this morning!' There's nothing more revealing than getting the bus into a city centre at 7.30am. Firstly, there's your driver – usually in a mood and with good reason. Not only are passengers trying to pay for a 50p journey with a tenner, but the poor man or woman has to look at the miserable faces of the rest of us as we get on and off. Miserable faces buried in books or phones or staring desperately out of the window or at the floor. Anything rather than look at anyone else. And the silence broken only by the rumble of the engine. In my commuter days I often wondered: What does the day promise for all these people I see? What does it promise for me?

The truth is that it's easier to have low expectations of the new day – of life. Isn't it safer to hope for little than to hope for much? To treat the promise of the new day with nothing more than the wish that we'll get through it with as little fuss as possible. If, then, it's difficult to face the promise of a new day, how much more difficult is it for us, at this time of year, to take hold of the promises described by Isaiah or John the Baptist. For if Advent and these passages are about anything, they're about promises, hope and expectation. Promises greater than most of us are ready to take hold of.

It's easy to miss how shocking the passage from Isaiah is. It's one of those bits of the Bible that gets read often enough for us to ignore its power. We've heard phrases like 'wolves and sheep will live together in peace' so often that we take them for granted. The enormous promises of God expressed in Isaiah become like a comfortable pair of old slippers we barely notice. In fact, the king, the Messiah, promised in Isaiah is so remarkable we can barely get our heads around the idea. The coming Messiah, in Isaiah, will not only judge wisely and defend the helpless – make the world a fair and decent place – but will transform the world beyond belief. I know many parents who are scared to let their kids play outside, but this passage promises that children will play with venomous snakes.

I don't sit comfortably with Isaiah's words. I know a lot of people who are experiencing life as an endless wilderness of austerity and marginalisation. If justice is shaped around a preferential option for the vulnerable and excluded, then justice is surely being withheld. The wealthy are only getting wealthier and a rich nation like the United Kingdom seems only to be making ever more strenuous efforts to treat people like the poor and asylum-seekers as scum. The world that the West has created – a series of failed states from West Africa through to the Middle East and beyond – is a world without obvious justice and in which even good-hearted Westerners are utterly complicit.

There are times when I want to ask this: if Jesus truly was the Messiah, the one who fulfilled Isaiah's prophecy, then why is the world still such a mess? What transformation of the world has his coming brought about? How is the Kingdom here present? It's tempting to answer this question by looking beyond the here and now to the promise of the Second Coming. To say, 'Yes the world's a mess, but don't worry, all we need to do is wait for Christ to come again and the Kingdom will be brought in.' Tempting perhaps, but I don't think it'll do. Jesus tells us that in him the Kingdom is already with us, even if it is still to come. And anyway, he also says that when he returns we'll be asked to give an account of our actions. If there's one thing that's certain, if you spend all your time looking to the future, you'll get nothing done now.

I'd suggest that part of the answer to my question, as to how Jesus the Messiah transforms the world, lies in the way he comes to the world and the way he dies. At Christmas we remember that the promised king, the Messiah, comes to us not as a warlord, astride a chariot or a tank, not as a powerful superhero, but as a vulnerable baby in need of loving care. God comes to us in need of our help. He calls us out to help him, to place ourselves in service of the vulnerable. God is helpless to act without our assistance. And that is the way of the Kingdom. And as Christ's death demonstrates, neither the world nor we can expect to be comfortable with this way of living. God does not promise us an easy time.

What am I suggesting here? Perhaps an example might help – unsurprisingly, a bus example. During one of my endless commutes in my pre-ordination days, I was travelling back from work up the Wilmslow Road in Manchester, exhausted and desperate for home, when I heard a heavily accented voice from the other side of the bus ask the person next to me, 'Can you tell me where Marks & Spencer's is?' The young woman hurriedly replied, 'I'm sorry, I don't know.' Out of the corner of my eye I saw that the questioner was the middle-aged South Asian man who'd got on the bus with his wife a few stops before.

I remember he'd had difficulty asking for the right ticket and I'd thought, 'Oh, for God's sake just hurry up, I want get home today.' As I sat there, I knew full well that the woman next to me knew exactly where M & S was. She just couldn't be bothered helping the bloke. And of course I, like almost everyone else, knew where M & S was. And to my shame, I thought, 'Leave the man and his wife to it. They'll easily find directions. I just don't need the hassle. I've spent half the day talking to strangers, I don't need two more.'

And, if I'm honest, there was a nasty bit of prejudice hanging around at the back of my mind – here was a Muslim couple, probably asylum-seekers, in search of help and my misguided dislike for Islam was in danger of being projected onto them. But most of all I couldn't be bothered.

Something stopped me from ignoring them – maybe what in *Star Wars* they'd call 'the Force', but what I'd call 'the Spirit'. I leant across, looked into the man's desperate eyes and said, 'I'll show you where M & S is,' planning just to point the couple in the right direction once we got off the bus at Piccadilly Gardens.

Ultimately I couldn't just do that. I couldn't just point my finger in the direction of Market Street and abandon them. I ended up walking the couple to M & S's door. During our five-minute walk I discovered, through a mixture of gestures and good-natured attempts at conversation, that the couple were over from Pakistan visiting the man's brother and were desperate to visit 'the famous M & S' to buy some underwear before returning home. We talked of cricket and food and I ended up with an invitation to visit them any time I happened to be in Pakistan.

Encounters like that are always unexpected and, I think, always change us. The couple told me they'd not expected such 'hospitality' in the UK – that someone would walk the extra distance with them. And, in truth, I hadn't expected to do so. I hadn't expected to be changed by offering someone directions, but somehow I was. As I'd got on the bus that morning, I'd hoped only for a nice easy day, but I got so much more because I'd taken the risk of opening myself to other possibilities and then acted on them. And maybe that's all God asks us to do. To open our eyes to the possibilities in his World. And what can we see when we do so? That Christ comes as a vulnerable child into this world, like a stranger from another land asking for help, inviting us to act on his behalf. Inviting us to discover the Kingdom here, now, on a bus or in the street – wherever. Let us pray that the Spirit will enable us to do so.

ENCOUNTERING THE DANGEROUS GOD

It has to be said – God can be very, very curious indeed. He seems to pick the oddest, most unexpected people for his service. Think of Moses – the cowardly runaway sent back to bring God's people out of slavery. Or Jonah who also runs away. And so on and so forth. Sometimes you have to think, 'Couldn't he do a lot better?' And then we come to Mary.

Consider Mary's encounter with Gabriel. Gabriel says, 'Greetings, favoured one! The Lord is with you.' The text suggests that Mary is perplexed and bewildered by this greeting, perhaps even suspicious of it. It is clear that, insofar as she is being invited to respond, she is uncertain how to do so. Mary senses risk and danger and disruption in God's approach. However we interpret what comes next, it is clear her instinct is right: for not only is she told that she is favoured by God but that she is going to have a God-blessed son, the result of being 'overshadowed' by the power of the Holy Spirit. And yet, as she points out, she is a 'virgin' and someone who has not known a man. She may be betrothed to Joseph, but (on the basis of the language Luke uses) is quite possibly a girl who hasn't yet had her first period. What response does this child make? 'Here am I, the servant of the Lord; let it be with me according to the word.'

There is simply no doubt that, textually, the images created by this encounter are troubling. A girl meeting God is one thing; a girl being told she will conceive a son via the 'overshadowing' power of the Holy Spirit is another. If this is God's call, then it is certainly intrusive, verging on the abusive: power is massively skewed towards God and the whole scene gives the impression of a *fait accompli*. And yet the writer of Luke makes Mary's response significant; Mary's willingness to unite her will and purposes to those of God is no mere afterthought.

Even if we imagine this angelic message delivered gently, there is no obvious gentleness in it. This call seems lacking in choice; the mood is imperative – 'You will ...' This God who chooses Mary comes to her dangerously and edgily. This is not a polite or nice God, but a God of expectations. His expectations go ahead of those he comes to, as if waiting for them to catch up.

I have perhaps not sketched the most attractive picture of God's calling. This is an overpowering, terrifying, insistent God who chooses individuals and expects obedience. An uncompromising God, who like an intrusive and over-confident parent presumes to know what is best for his children and who may value our response, but expects that response to be 'Yes'.

This is a God I instinctively want to speak against. I want to pile up counter-cases against this God's behaviour – emphasising the compassion, gentleness and generosity of God. And yet there is something in this picture I've sketched that I want to take seriously – that both resonates in experience and is actually worthy of deep spiritual consideration.

There is an authenticity to this alien God. This is no domesticated, easy God; this is almost certainly not the kind of God that one would invent for one's own comfort. This God is neither a comfort blanket nor a consumer accessory adopted in order to make one's life feel complete. In an age in which the God who is often preached is one who is gentle, friendly and not overly demanding, this is a God who is alien and strange. And yet faithful. This is no Greek god, full of bewildering, yet very human, caprice.

In Scorsese's *The Last Temptation of Christ*, Jesus' opening line is 'God loves me. I know God loves me. I wish he'd stop.' There is something of this in the kind of God who meets Mary. This is the God who calls but who also pushes us out so very far from our ordinary human desires and expectations. This is the God who drives Jesus out into the wilderness, who expects Jesus' followers to take up the Cross and follow him, and who leads Jesus on that bleak road to Jerusalem. This is the God who fills Mary's heart full of rejoicing and yet gifts her a son who pierces her heart. This is the God who is with Moses and yet is behind mass slaughter, who pushes his chosen people out into the wilderness for countless years. And somewhere in all this bleakness, in this wilderness and so much night, is the mystery of Love.

We are all called, and calling really matters, because it indicates a way of living that resists certain modern pictures of who we should be. These pictures are inclined to view us as individualised economic units whose main purpose is to maintain a reasonable level of existence for ourselves and ensure that we are not too great a burden on a society comprised of individuals who come together merely for mutual benefit. In this picture, what matters most is not who we are, what gifts we have and to what we are drawn, but having a job. A society ordered on this kind of principle will be more concerned about how its citizens can be useful than in helping them discern what they are really about. The purpose of education will entail encouraging young people to pursue paths that are effective, economically successful and productive rather than seeking to help them figure out who they are, be attentive to what they are drawn to and discern what they are capable of.

For calling is about being drawn out of oneself towards something: a career, a way of life, of being. And so it is also about *response*. It requires commitment, a joining of one's will to that to which one is being drawn. It is about a 'yes' and then giving of ourselves to that direction. And it is never passive.

Travelling with God, then – the way of vocation – is never merely about a job or even a course of action. It is about the shape and direction of a life and accepting the prospect that this may change us – for either good or ill. We might even get bloody, but within it may lurk true blessing. It is not lifestyle – that great modern idea of what our jobs may allow us to lead – but living. And if God is the true ground of our being and the very heart of what we most truly are, her call will always be the primary one. When she comes calling, we may resist, be suspicious and so on, but we can be assured we are being drawn out into our deepest, truest selves.

A SERMON FOR CHRISTMAS NIGHT

Here we are on Christmas night – perhaps *the* most joyous night of the year, a night of wonder and peace – and though we celebrate, there are so many bleak places, physically and emotionally speaking, to be found on this globe. How much joy will people in Syria be experiencing tonight? Or how much peace and goodwill is there in Iraq or Burma? To bring things nearer home, how many streets would you have to travel to find someone weeping? There are so many people separated from their loved ones, so many people home-less, or fleeing from persecution. Poverty, marginalisation and isolation are part of our lived reality. That old Christmas song 'It'll be lonely this Christmas without you to hold' is cheesy but I'm sure there are many people without loved ones who feel more or less that way.

How can we affirm that this holiest of nights is the most joyous night of the year? It is over 2000 years now since Jesus Christ was born and yet there is just as much war, the gap between poor and rich grows wider, and we seem more inured to conspicuous consumption than ever. As I've wandered through Manchester these past few days I have seen little evidence of Christmas cheer and rejoicing. Everyone seems weighed down with the cold and with the need to make sure they've got the right amount of bacon and sausage rolls or their veggie alternative for Christmas dinner. And I've been left asking, why do we do it to ourselves? Where is Christmas in all this? Has it indeed just become another means to oppress ourselves? Where, in the midst of our bruised and broken world, is the Christ Child, the Prince of Peace, Wonderful Counsellor, King of Kings, Almighty God and Lover of our Souls? I, like many of you, am well capable of doubting that this God who was to save is to be found anywhere.

But after all our doubts and raging have burned out, after our adult intellects have interrogated the world and found little evidence, indeed few rumours, of the God who saves, we return to the mystery of the gospels and discover that it is in the form of a helpless baby that God – the Very Love which illuminates an otherwise compromised and frightening world – has crept in beside us. And I can't emphasise enough how this is not just some fairy story or fodder for the kids. This story of God coming to us as one of us, as a babe in arms who needs almost constant support, who could be abandoned, who could be abused, who elicits such primitive love and humanity, is the most important story in the world. For this is God breaking down all the barriers we erect – between religion, race, culture, class – and inviting us to respond at the most basic level: that of love for another vulnerable human being who, without our tender care, will die and be lost. In the end, it is only this love which will save us.

The heart of the Christmas message shakes us free from the sentimentality which clogs up our veins as surely as all those mince pies. It is a message about where God is to be found. For if you and I were to search for him, perhaps we'd go to the glamorous places – to palaces where the rich and famous hang out. For surely God is the most powerful and famous of all. He'd be hanging out with his celebrity mates. But if we went there, he'd be nowhere to be found. Maybe we'd go searching in the holy places of the world – surely we'd find him in a magnificent place of worship like St Pauls' or Chartres. Somewhere grand and dedicated to the glory of God. But I don't think we'd find him hanging out there much either – though I'm sure he appreciates all our singing and love.

The truth is that Christmas invites us to find God in the most compromised and difficult places. Not in palaces or temples but among those reduced to sharing the birth of their firstborn with animals, without home, barely with shelter. And I do not think that on that first Christmas night Jesus was like the child in *Away in a Manger* – 'Little Lord Jesus no crying he makes'. Real kids ain't like that; and I think Jesus was the most real person who ever lived. I suspect he cried. But his tears were for all those who are bereaved; for all those who had ever been made to feel stupid or small; for all the bullied, the despised and abused and friendless. Jesus – God – weeps in solidarity with a compromised world.

If there is hope in this, the hope lies in God's trust in us. He trusts us to pick him up – to pick up all those who have been dumped on by life – and hold him and love him, until he begins to laugh again. Only a baby possesses in a truly uncompromised way this laughter of pure delight and joy. The joy of the world. That is our blessed calling – to pick up God this night and always, and wipe away his tears and help him to laugh again. To stand in solidarity – and active solidarity – with a world that is restless for love and hungry for justice. And then our joy shall be great and God's love will be known.

ANOTHER CHRISTMAS TALK

It is so easy for us to forget Joseph isn't it? According to the Bible he's not even the biological father of Jesus. We're told that when he finds out that Mary is pregnant he thinks about breaking off with her – though, in his cultural context, that is not an entirely incomprehensible action. The nativity can seem to be all about Mary and the angels and the shepherds and most of all 'the baby Jesus'. The whole scene sometimes seems cartoonish, a kitsch performance of sickly sentiment. Joseph – represented as an old man caught up in events he cannot begin to understand – is at the margins of a picture that has a smiling Jesus and adoring Mary at the centre. In so many ways Joseph is an everyman and, indeed, an everywoman. He is the person who, like so many of us, is present in a situation but is not the centre of attention. He is the one on the edge. He is the one no one seems to take much notice of.

Where do we see ourselves in the world? We are all, I suggest, a mixture of the truly remarkable and the very ordinary. Perhaps some of us occupy or have occupied very powerful and influential positions in life or will do one day. But even so, how difficult it can seem to make a difference, to bring about change. We are all very aware, I trust, of the places where there is no peace tonight, where people across the world have very little or live in fear. Even the most powerful often feel impotent in the face of so much need – left on the sidelines, looking on. Indeed I have spoken to politicians who have admitted that on approaching the summit of power they have been shocked to discover the extent to which their hands are tied. How much more so for us, then.

Like Joseph, do we need a second chance at life? The older I get, the more I realise I need not just a second or third or even a fourth chance, but countless chances. Because, frankly, living life and indeed trying to live it well involves making countless mistakes. Don't let anyone tell you otherwise. And all we can hope for is that our judgement and luck are such that the errors we make are not too disastrous or damaging. Sometimes it's very hard not to look back on choices and decisions with regret, to imagine that life was easier or simpler in the past.

Ultimately, Jesus Christ – the God who risks everything to be with us as one of us – is all about second chances. For imagine living in a world where everyone had to be perfect, could not take risks, could not make mistakes; where we were condemned as soon as we made a wrong step. How long would even the best of us last? We are all compromised. We are all people of unclean hands and unclean lips. Without grace and forgiveness and love we would be totally lost.

Jesus is grace and forgiveness and love – and therefore hope. He is the one who exposes a ruthless world for what it is and shows us another way. He calls us out of ourselves to demonstrate love for the weakest and most vulnerable – for the ones who are like babies in our arms. Joseph – the forgotten man – is an icon of grace. He offers a template for masculine performance that is not predicated on anxiety. For the choice presented to the Joseph of our nativity stories is pretty stark. He can choose a patriarchally sanctioned rejection of Mary on grounds that – by her own admission – she is pregnant by someone else. She has entered a contract of commitment with him but has reneged on that commitment. In order to maintain his status and power, the patriarchal system would support Joseph's rejection of her, apportioning blame on Mary's side and leaving him unsullied.

However, if Joseph chooses to remain faithful to Mary he lays himself open to suggestions that he has behaved inappropriately. The implication would be that the child is his and he has had conjugal relations ahead of a formal sanction of his union. If that brings his status into question, how much more so for his intended? Mary can be scapegoated as a person who 'gives it out' before the relationship has been legalised. Together they might be quietly treated as different, as marginal. They would have to negotiate the gossip and innuendo of small town and village life.

But there are other things at stake too. Psychologically, when Joseph makes his commitment to Mary, he is committing to a child he knows is not his. In a patriarchally shaped culture, he is stepping outside the pride and security of paternity and lineage. Sons are prized over daughters, but what is truly prized is a boy who can demonstrate he is genuinely his father's son. Indeed, one dimension of the genealogy contained in Matthew's gospel is to ensure that Jesus' forebears are properly asserted. (An exciting aspect of that genealogy is how it occasionally departs from the male line and includes women like Ruth.)

So Joseph's commitment to a child that is not directly his own, and to a woman whom he might legitimately have abandoned, is an extraordinary and exciting subversion of the patriarchy implicit in the situation. Joseph's trust and commitment, ultimately to God, is a rejection of a conception of masculinity that is so unsure of itself that it has to define its borders carefully. Joseph's identity is not dependent on being assured of his paternity of Jesus. He commits to a son who is not biologically his. Nor does it depend on having a wife whose status is above question or innuendo. He takes the power and position given to him in virtue of his status as a man and places it into radical question and into dangerous space. In short, he takes the risk of letting his masculinity be interrogated and remade by a radical God.

A TONKA TOY CHRISTMAS

I don't usually remember individual childhood Christmases. Like overused plasticine, all the distinctive colours blend into one mud-brown. And in most respects Christmas day 1975 was not, by my family's 1970s' experience, a particularly unusual Christmas. We were still very poor, a largish family cramped into a three-bedroom semi-detached house, huddling around one coal fire for warmth during the day, we children getting lost in the deep polyester caverns of our sleeping bags at night. And yet this 'Tonka toy Christmas' glows yellow and black, roars like a 50-ton truck; it defines my childhood. Its importance lies in the iconic nature of the indestructible Tonka truck that I was given and adored. It was moulded plastic, but hard as nails. Its unbreakable shiny newness revealed, to a five-year-old, one of the faces of God. I straddled its black driver's cab and trundled off down the hall to the soundtrack of my own satisfyingly throaty chug.

This was, for me, the ultimate boy toy – more macho than Action Man's scar, bolder than Evel Knievel, better able to come back for more punishment than the Six Million Dollar Man. And the fact that I had one at five has rebounded, like a ball in a pinball machine, through my Christmases and my life ever since. For although one might argue that nothing could be more appropriate for a five-year-old working-class boy than a yellow dumper truck, there was one problem: this five-year-old boy wanted, at a profound but hardly articulated level, to be a girl. But, even as a five-year-old, I was desperate for no one to glimpse – even catch a peek through my closed-fingered defences – this truth about me. No one must know. Ever. And so the ultimate boy toy was the perfect present. That Tonka toy Christmas, I see now, symbolised and anticipated my life for the next 16 years. For, as I grew up and became ever more aware of my gender dysphoria, the more I sought to conceal it. How better, especially at Christmas, than to behave in ways that signify 'boy' and 'masculinity'? Even now, many years on from my gender change, I still work through the implications of the commitments I made at the age of five and it is Christmas which provides the focus for this. For not only is it the part of the year when I typically spend an extended period with my immediate family, but it is a time of intense sharing and scrutiny.

Being a transsexual child is, by its very nature, uncomfortable, especially in a claustrophobic village where granny is twitching the curtain every five minutes to check you're behaving correctly. This was especially true in an age when the only press about 'sex changes' was confined to tabloid sensationalism. But discomfort doesn't prevent a small child from living, from trying to make the best of things. The ache of discomfort, of dysphoria, was simply that: an ache. And I became superb at disguise, pretending to be a perfectly ordinary boy and teenager. Sometimes, and typically at Christmas, that ache coalesced with other factors – choosing what presents to have, family expectations – into a painful knotty blockage. A cyst. The cyst grew fat and bloated and harder to disguise. I tried to ignore it. My teenage years were marked not only with the usual adolescent malaise of confusion and body discomfort experienced by almost everyone, but were also attended by horror at what my body was becoming and an inability to talk about this to anyone. Christmas 1990 was the logical, painful culmination of a process that had begun with the Tonka toy Christmas fifteen years before. For in 1975 I'd committed myself to being a 'normal little boy'; the Tonka toy was the sacramental sealing of that commitment. My resolution had just enough energy to last fifteen years. In 1990, in a state of depression, as I lay awake in bed in the early hours of Christmas day, I tried to renew the covenant, this time in the form of a prayer – a prayer to myself, to whatever God I believed in, to the God of hopeless causes. I couldn't stand the thought of being true to myself and I was desperate to avoid hurting my parents. I would, then, be heroic: I would embrace this hairy, muscly creature I'd grown into and live as a happy man – at least until such a time as everyone whom I might hurt by changing sex had died off. My 20-year-old self was superb at making grand gestures. This final gesture had momentum enough to keep me in public denial for another two years. At the end of that time I could no longer avoid the truth. The grand gesture collapsed. My family/friends and I began to talk, really talk. I dropped the little boy hands from my eyes and peeked out, allowing myself to be looked upon, really looked upon, for the first time. I began the difficult and remarkable journey of changing sex.

Much of my early life was a process of being silenced – partly through conscious self-silencing, partly through the absorption of family, social and cultural mores. I could find no language in which to speak through taboos about gender identity. So I settled into silence. Silence – and breaking out of it – has been a key trope of my life. It is intriguing that so much personal silence has coalesced around my experience of Christmas. Perhaps inevitably, as someone who is both a priest and a theologian, I've wanted to interrogate the Nativity narratives in an attempt to locate myself within them. 'Who,' I've wanted to ask, 'represents the silenced in these narratives? Who represents the likes of me?' The answers to this question provide some of the theological sense I can find in Christmas from a transgendered perspective. Part of me is happy simply to ask the question and allow it to resonate; part of me wants to shake it like a Christmas tree, hoping that hidden gifts and treasure will fall out. If my Christmases (and my broader life) have typically been characterised by silence, how does God speak into that? When I read the gospels I am immediately struck by the fact that two of them – Mark and John – basically lack Christmas narratives. This is, no doubt, for all sorts of reasons, but I find this absence *as absence* both striking and strangely encouraging; it is as if Jesus himself has lost his nativity, his origins, his childhood. It has been silenced because it has not been included. Or to come at it another way: the wholeness of Jesus is not compromised because a childhood or birth narrative has been omitted. Jesus is whole – even as much of his story is silenced. Even in Matthew and Luke – which have Christmas narratives – I'm struck by the swathes of silence. In Luke, once Mary has made her extraordinary *Magnificat,* she becomes, effectively, a silent figure. Perhaps the writer of Luke, writing in a prophetic rather than a literary voice, feels that the birth itself speaks enough. But it is as if the birth silences Mary. Equally, the baby Jesus is unconvincingly silent. There is no account of crying. Some will respond by saying that the lack of crying is irrelevant – after all, the gospel is not a novel, but a work of prophetic and apocalyptic literature. But still the absence of any reference to this basic human noise allows the space for the kind of sentimental Victorian 'Away in a Manger' Jesus ('little Lord Jesus, no crying he makes') to emerge. Except I do not read this silence as evidence of virtue; it is evidence of Christ's identification with the silenced. This is a God who has not yet discovered his voice. This unpromising, perhaps ignominious, beginning for God-With-Us is taboo-cracking. What kind of God gets born in an outhouse? What kind of God invites the despised (such as shepherds) to his nativity? What kind of God becomes one of the silenced? In the beginning may have been the Word; but the Word in the Nativity cannot yet speak itself. I suspect some transgendered people will find their experience of being silenced most resonates with that of the so-called Holy Innocents; that their silence is not temporary, waiting to be overcome. Their voices have been cut off (by societal/cultural/personal pressures) as permanently as the lives of Herod's victims. But that is not my story. My voice may be hidden, but I'm learning to speak. As Christ had to find his voice, so am I on a journey to find mine.

Life is different for me now and, inevitably, so is Christmas. When I woke up to the fact that public denial would not do, when I realised the unsustainability of grand gestures, I began the slow and sometimes painfully confusing process of 'changing gender'. It was a risky but ultimately correct decision. My family have been tremendously supportive and, perhaps, delightfully surprised – they have unexpectedly gained a sister, daughter and aunt. But the cost for us all has also been massive, and Christmas remains a kind of gathering up of both the joy and the cost. The joy lies in relationships reshaped and relaxed; in the discovery, in the midst of the ordinary annual gathering of family, of the absurd, unexpected grace of God. Grace signified by the absurdity of God being born in an outhouse in Bethlehem among nobodies and the disreputable. The cost is wrapped up in a new kind of silence, with an extra layer added each year. It is a silence no one in particular has made, but which impacts on all my family, most particularly my parents. For one of the costs of my emergent identity has been to make it difficult for my family to speak confidently about my early life as a boy and young man. There is a sense in which, for my family as a whole, my early life has been lost.[1]

This is a kind of journey into darkness – a darkness that is just as positive as it may appear negative. The choices I have made – like all real choices – have closed down certain possibilities. However, unlike many choices, mine have closed down or at least made very difficult some of the discourses families take for granted: the chewing over and celebrating of all sorts of details of childhood. It is as if a light on the past has been switched off. There is an absence. A silence. A darkness.

When I am in a one-to-one with my parents or siblings, things can be different. I have always tried to encourage my family members to feel they can celebrate (rather than feel shame about) my early life. I try to integrate my whole life into who I am now and recognise that there is much in my pre-sex-change worth celebrating – but the weight of being together *en masse* makes the public acknowledgement of my past difficult. This is particularly the case when my siblings' children are present – children who have only ever known me as 'Auntie Rachel'. I sense the difficulty in acknowledging my past has something to do with the social nature of Christmas: the present is important, but much of Christmas is memory and remembrance. Perhaps, in time, my family and I shall discover, like a delightfully unexpected present, a way through this new silence, this new darkness. And, if we do not, then I'm encouraged by the thought that silence and darkness are not, in themselves, terrible things.

As for the Tonka truck of 1975, well, it is long gone, perhaps suffering the slow, stench-filled decomposition that plastic and metal undergo in a landfill waste site. But in my head it is still with me, though I have become aware of how, in recent Christmases, I have been slowly dismantling this once indestructible toy, piece by piece, wheel by wheel, sometimes with care, sometimes with abandon. And each loosened bolt and nut is a making vulnerable, a loosening of false layers of identity, and a making space for God, the one who is easily silenced, to speak. As such, it is thus an embracing of God's darkness – profound, fecund, full of endless possibility and creativity.

---

[1] As one friend has pointed out, this experience of 'loss' is perhaps far more common than many would prefer to believe. Families represent one of the key theatres of human living and thus will inevitably be the loci of some of our bleaker dramas.

A JOYLESS CHRISTMAS

It was the night before Christmas and all through the house not a creature was stirring, not even a mouse. Well, no one – no man, no woman, no child – dared. The consequences might be terrible. This year there would be no stockings, no decorations, no singing, no carousing. Anyone found in a state of excitement or over-indulgence this night and in the coming days would be in danger of severe punishment. As the day of our Lord's birth arrived, the brave whispered 'Happy Christmas' to each other, and sent invites to secret festivities. For there was great fear of getting caught. For this year Christmas was cancelled by order of Parliament.

The year is 1647 – when Oliver Cromwell persuaded Parliament to ban Christmas. It was not, I suggest, one of the highlights of English history. Cromwell and his Puritan Party have forever since been associated with misery and bah humbug. He is, in the English imagination, the original Scrooge. One could almost hear him, two centuries before Dickens' Scrooge, saying, 'Every idiot who goes about with "Merry Christmas" on his lips should be boiled with his own pudding, and buried with a stake of holly in his heart." Yet, the truth was that Cromwell wanted people to get back to the real meaning of the holy day when the birth of the Saviour of the world was commemorated. He, like so many politicians since, despised and legislated against the alcohol-induced excesses of the English; and we all know how heartily the English, let alone the Welsh, Scots and Irish, like a drink.

For Cromwell was deeply anxious that the British traditions of partying and carousing at Christmas time lacked respect for the true meaning of Christmas. These themes of anxiety about the real meaning of Christmas and concern for the moral behaviour of one's neighbour at this time of year are both depressingly and reassuringly contemporary. Should you pick up certain newspapers, listen to radio or watch TV news programmes you might be left believing that the UK is in a state of panic about the meaning of Christmas – brought to the brink of fisticuffs by rampant secularists who want to rebrand Christmas as 'Winterval' or pagans in search of Saturnalia or Yule. We live in a society where, many believe, a new God has risen and he is a tyrant and his name is Consumerism, and should you incur his wrath by turning your face against him, then you will be unloved and alone at Christmas; for unless you spend your heart out on others, you can expect nothing in return. You are what you spend; the Christian God is dead; long live the God of Money!

To discover that the meaning and place of Christmas as a religious festival has long been open to negotiation can help calm us in the face of media hype and moral panic about the direction of our society. The way we 'do' Christmas, as many of you will know, is a juicy mixture of pagan, Christian and, crucially, Germanic traditions imported into the UK in the 19th century by Queen Victoria's husband, Prince Albert. And, though many of us may be uncomfortable about conspicuous consumption, we should be careful about pious pronouncements about how 'they' – meaning the so-called non-religious - 'do' Christmas. 'If only we could get back to the real meaning of Christmas,' we might say, but we are all complicit in a society so laden down with material wealth that we no longer understand that Advent is a time of fasting in preparation for the true feast of Christmas.

Then again, we face Christmas under new circumstances. We have learned new phrases in recent years like 'credit crunch' and 'fiscal austerity' and perhaps lots of us are learning to be a bit more careful with our money. Maybe these new circumstances, difficult as they are for many of us, will be an opportunity for us to rediscover a simpler Christmas stripped of some of the layers of flummery we have wrapped around it. And let us not forget those for whom this Christmas will feel pretty empty and meaningless because a loved one has departed or they simply have no one to celebrate with. In their company, we should be careful about pronouncing on the real meaning of Christmas.

Equally, we should dare to be critical of the narrative of austerity that is being propagated by some of the wealthiest and most privileged in the land. The rhetoric of 'we're all in this together' has worn pretty thin, when some with already considerable political and economic power are making killings on the markets and living lives of conspicuous consumption, whilst their economics have led to exponential growth in the numbers of homeless people and food bank users. If God is calling us to live a Christmas stripped of flummery, part of that is surely seeing things clearly and as they are, without any childish rhetoric. Let us dare to see reality as it is, for that is where God is, struggling to reveal good news for some and critique for others.

If Christmas has always been complicated, multi-layered and comprised of many meanings, then can we talk about the true meaning of Christmas? And could we bear its truth if we did find it? Perhaps we should learn simply to let the Christmas story speak for itself and be happy with that. For the mystery, the truth, the beauty and hope of Christmas are embedded in nothing more or less than the simple story we have in the gospels. And though we have overlaid it with centuries of kitsch, sentiment, even campness, the nativity of Christ has an extraordinary vulnerable power.

The God revealed by the mystery of Christmas is not the God of tyrants. The God shown at Christmas is not one of neo-liberal austerity – he is born poor not to ensure that those who are already wealthy become richer, but to call us to account for our cravenness and call us into abundant love. He does not insist that we worship him in particular ways, only that we protect him. He puts himself, like all newborns, utterly in our hands. The trust placed in us is complete. We shall have to teach him to speak, to socialise, to live and to love.

The Christian God is outrageous. He says, in effect, I love you so much that I trust you to be responsible, to be grown-ups. I shall not treat you like little children; I shall not insist that you behave in this way or that; I shall not be like the many 'isms' – capitalism, consumerism, and so on – which you create in order to regulate your lives and which become monsters you cannot control. I come as a baby – who must be fed, cleaned and changed, who cries, who can be ignored, pushed aside, mistreated.

If God dares to come to us so boldly, so vulnerably, so strangely, should we be surprised that he gets so easily overlooked, misunderstood or sentimentalised? This is a God who is so insanely trusting that he lets us set the agenda. Christmas is, ironically, about us – the human race; but in an unusual way. It is an invitation to stop being self-centred and self-sufficient. It is an invitation to discover who we truly are in loving someone totally dependent on us, and utterly vulnerable. The invitation is freely offered. Will your love be set alive in response to a baby born in an obscure village in the company of peasants, the unwashed and the insignificant? Behold the face of love shown in a baby – not the sentimental half-love we seem to specialise in, in our modern world, but the immensely demanding love that invites us to stand up, be responsible and show our solidarity with the God who awaits discovery in the vulnerable of our local town, the Congo, Bethlehem, the world, this night and always.

I can be a bit of a misery guts about Christmas. I sometimes worry that Cromwell, Scrooge and the Grinch are my spiritual friends. But we should not be afraid to feast at Christmas. For the wondrously trusting God who shares himself utterly with us invites us to do the same with each other. So let us rejoice and make a feast of ourselves this Christmas time. Have a joyous, peaceful and loving Christmastide.

WILD GOOSE PUBLICATIONS IS PART OF THE IONA COMMUNITY ...

- An ecumenical movement of men and women from different walks of life and different traditions in the Christian church
- Committed to the gospel of Jesus Christ, and to following where that leads, even into the unknown
- Engaged together, and with people of goodwill across the world, in acting, reflecting and praying for justice, peace and the integrity of creation
- Convinced that the inclusive community we seek must be embodied in the community we practise

Together with our staff, we are responsible for:

- Our islands residential centres of Iona Abbey, the MacLeod Centre on Iona, and Camas Adventure Centre on the Ross of Mull

and in Glasgow:

- The administration of the Community
- Our work with young people
- Our publishing house, Wild Goose Publications
- Our association in the revitalising of worship with the Wild Goose Resource Group

The Iona Community was founded in Glasgow in 1938 by George MacLeod, minister, visionary and prophetic witness for peace, in the context of the poverty and despair of the Depression. Its original task of rebuilding the monastic ruins of Iona Abbey became a sign of hopeful rebuilding of community in Scotland and beyond. Today, we are about 280 Members, mostly in Britain, and 1500 Associate Members, with 1400 Friends worldwide. Together and apart, 'we follow the light we have, and pray for more light'.

For information on the Iona Community contact:
The Iona Community, 21 Carlton Court, Glasgow G5 9JP, UK. Phone: 0141 429 7281
e-mail: admin@iona.org.uk; web: www.iona.org.uk

For enquiries about visiting Iona, please contact:
Iona Abbey, Isle of Iona, Argyll PA76 6SN, UK. Phone: 01681 700404
e-mail: ionacomm@iona.org.uk